Power X Change

Brittany Lee

Dedication

I probably learned more about myself during this journey that lasted about 20 years. The impact I left on the minds and hearts of the men I encountered during my time as Mistress Raven has shaped who I am today.

What began as a way to understand my husband's hidden desires ended up opening my once-naive mind and unlocking my own Pandora's Box. I feel as if I have lived two totally different lives in the years I have been on the earth. Each had its benefits as well as disadvantages. I'm still the same woman, but my experiences in both worlds formed my current mindset.

Regrets? Of course, but who doesn't have any? In the grand scheme, my experiences have evolved into the woman who I'm proud to say is ME. I would be remiss if I didn't acknowledge the most influential individuals who affected my journey.

The first life (I have lived two) is credited to my parents. Their unconditional love and support molded the girl and then the woman I became. Their philosophy, which was set by example, was always to be kind.

Volunteerism is in my blood. Helping others who were less fortunate or possibly ill appeared to me as a need to do whatever I could to help. My father was my hero. As I mentioned in this book, he died in my arms in an elevator of the building where his law offices were at the age of 63... alone together on the floor.

That very day, we had put a deposit at Tavern on The Green in Central Park for my wedding to my husband, to whom I have been married for 46 years now, from joy to unmitigated pain. My life would never be the same.

Those feelings and images still haunt me today.

At the age of 44, that woman was reborn as Mistress Raven. That creation was actually foisted upon me as I learned of my husband's double life. I threw myself into this new, unfamiliar world, absorbing all its strange details and trying to make sense of it all.

In 2020, I met a producer named Harris Salomon, who was impressed with me, and we forged a partnership pursuing various projects. His importance during this new life was essential. Though the avenues we attempted to navigate did not come to fruition, his support gave me a great deal of confidence.

My husband is actually the person who felt my story needed to be told. He obviously is the motivation for the existence of the character Mistress Raven.

Nick Broomfield, the Peabody-winning documentarian who directed Fetishes for HBO, revealed my secret to the rest of the world. I became somewhat of a reluctant celebrity. Famous or infamous, journalists from cities globally were contacting me.

Many lives experienced various iterations. However, mine has a pronounced divide... before and after.

Finally, I need to add that some of the women whom I hired to work at Pandoras Box affected me deeply. I have even resurrected a long-distance relationship with one. The men who were my clients, besides helping them with their psychological needs, taught me a great deal about myself.

Acknowledgment

iii

I can't overlook the most influential people in my journey, my parents, who shaped my first life. Their unconditional love and support molded me from a girl into the woman I became. Through their actions, they taught me to always be kind.

Contents

Preface

From the earliest moments of my life as a dutiful daughter, I felt a constant need to please those around me. My love for my family pushed me to seek their approval, unknowingly starting a lifelong struggle. With every step I took, I longed to be seen as worthy and hoped to be appreciated for my dedication. From a very young age, it had been instilled in me to seek approval—the chain started with my parents, who were both successful, well-respected individuals. Their accomplishments cast long shadows that I yearned to step into, to prove myself worthy of their love and pride. Their achievements seemed like guiding lights, and I believed that by achieving greatness myself, I would finally feel deserving of their admiration.

As I went through my early years, I became very aware of the unspoken expectations surrounding me. Every decision I made, every step I took, was colored by the desire to meet the lofty standards set for me. It wasn't merely about striving for success—it was about surpassing the predetermined high bar. I yearned to be seen as exceptional, as a reflection of the greatness my parents had achieved. Their approval became my measuring stick for self-worth, and I felt compelled to prove my capabilities continually.

But as I kept chasing perfection, I gradually realized that the finish line I'd been focused on wasn't real. No matter how much I accomplished or how many accolades I garnered, it seemed that the goalposts of approval were forever shifting. The more I pushed myself, the further away the validation seemed to slip. It was a disheartening revelation, an unwelcome truth that pierced my soul. The demands disguised as hopes placed upon me were insatiable, leaving me forever reaching, forever striving, and forever falling short.

The pressure to please extended beyond my immediate family. It permeated every facet of my life — from teachers and mentors to friends and romantic partners. I became adept at molding myself into the person I believed others wanted me to be. I longed to fit into the molds created for me, to be accepted and celebrated by those around me. I was deeply afraid of rejection, which pushed me to mold myself into others' expectations. Instead of staying true to my own desires and goals, I became what others wanted me to be.

As I transitioned into the role of an obedient wife, the threads of my people-pleasing nature grew stronger still. Fueled by an ardent desire to maintain harmony within my marriage, I constantly prioritized my partner's needs over my own. I surrendered my desires, molding myself into the role of the perfect spouse. Beneath my self-sacrifice, a storm was building, a mix of emotions and buried dreams. It grew stronger, threatening to overwhelm me.

Life became a collection of missed chances and unfulfilled dreams. Behind every smile I put on and every selfless act I did, there were hidden desires I had pushed aside. The weight of people's faith in me pressed down upon me, burying my own hopes and dreams beneath layers of self-neglect. My journey became a delicate balancing act, a constant tightrope walk between the happiness of others and the echoes of my own desires.

A quiet discontent sat beneath my carefully built exterior. I couldn't ignore the feeling inside me. The need to find my voice again and follow the dreams I had pushed aside for too long. It was a journey of self-discovery, unraveling the layers of conditioning and societal expectations that had held me captive for years.

This constant need for approval ended up being a double-edged sword. It pushed me to try harder but also brought its own set of struggles. On the one hand, it drove me to achieve remarkable feats and pushed me to excel in various aspects of my life. It propelled me forward, compelling me to explore my potential and strive for greatness. However, on the other hand, it also consumed me, gradually eroding my sense of self. I lost touch with my own desires and dreams, tethered to the whims and wishes of those I sought to please. I became like a chameleon, adjusting to the desires and wishes of others while my true self slowly faded into the background.

With each passing year, the weight of external validation grew heavier, burdening my spirit. The gap between who I really was and who I showed the world grew more and more unsettling. The smile I wore on my face masked the turmoil brewing within, the constant struggle between the person I longed to be and the person I felt I needed to be. The relentless pursuit of approval ensnared me in a cycle of never-ending comparison. It left me perpetually dissatisfied with my accomplishments and forever seeking appreciation from others.

This people-pleasing behavior led me on a roller coaster ride that became the very essence of my existence. It was a rocky journey, with exciting highs that felt like they reached the sky and crushing lows that sent me into deep despair. Like a perpetual cycle of euphoria and anguish, this ride consumed me, leaving an indelible mark on my soul.

The highs of this relentless quest for approval were truly intoxicating. When I succeeded in meeting the expectations of others, a euphoric rush would course through my veins. It was a thrilling experience, like a dance with success, an exciting rush that briefly filled the emptiness inside me. In those fleeting moments, I felt a surge of self-worth, a sense of purpose that momentarily silenced the whispers of doubt and insecurity.

But like any roller coaster, the thrilling highs were always followed by painful lows that dragged me into despair. The lows were a merciless onslaught of self-doubt, self-criticism, and a profound sense of inadequacy. The weight of real and perceived expectations bore down upon me, threatening to crush my spirit. In those moments of darkness, I questioned my worth, my abilities, and whether I would ever measure up to the impossibly high standards I had set for myself.

This roller coaster ride had profound effects on both my psyche and my brain chemistry. It rewired the very pathways of my mind, forging neural connections that perpetuated this cycle. It became a part of who I was, influencing my thoughts, feelings, and actions. I became caught in a feedback loop, where the pursuit of approval triggered the release of chemicals in my brain that reinforced this addictive pattern.

Even now, I'm still dealing with the consequences of this wild journey. I still can't tell if I became someone hooked on the adrenaline-filled highs, always seeking recognition from others, or if I became someone afraid of taking risks, reluctant to assert my own desires. Either way, I find myself stuck in between. The line between the two seems blurred, and I am left grappling with my own identity, uncertain of who I truly am beneath the layers of people-pleasing.

In the depths of my journey as a people pleaser, I realized that the true cost of seeking approval was the erosion of my own authenticity. I had lost sight of who I was beyond everyone's idea of me. My self-worth had become intrinsically tied to the opinions and approval of others, leaving me vulnerable to their judgments and critiques.

As I reflect upon the path I have traveled, I am filled with a mixture of emotions: a profound sense of yearning for freedom, a tinge of regret for the dreams left unfulfilled, and a growing resolve to reclaim my identity. This book explores the emotional journey that came from my lifelong search for approval. It reflects the strength of the human spirit as I start to uncover the true me, hidden beneath years of people-pleasing. It's about the process of rediscovering who I really am.

This story of pain and strength shows the power that comes when you finally face the damage caused by years of neglecting yourself. It is a journey of reclaiming my worthiness and learning to break free from the chains of external validation.

Within these words, you will find the universal struggles of finding one's true voice and the timeless quest for self-love and fulfillment. Through the pages of this book, I invite you to join me on a profound, introspective journey. Together, we will explore the depths of the emotions that entwine with the act of people pleasing — a delicate dance between the joy of making others happy and the pain of losing oneself in the process.

As I share my story, I invite you to join me in unraveling the intricate layers of this roller coaster ride. Let's explore the highs and lows together, looking at the effects of this constant chase for approval. In doing so, we may begin to untangle the complex web of emotions and uncover the path to liberation, which leads to self-acceptance, self-love, and the reclamation of our true selves. And who knows, maybe, like me, you might learn something from my journey and go from being controlled to being in control.

Chapter 1

In the story of our lives, our childhood is like a thread we are made up of; it is an integral part of our being, or in other words, it is who we are. The way we grow up, how are surroundings, especially our families, treat us, and all the little moments we share each day shape our personalities. No matter where we're from or which time we live in, how we are raised and the relationships we build when we're young deeply affect the people we become later on.

At an early age, we are not only influenced by our parents but in general, how the whole family behaved with us. Back then, it did not seem that important, but later on in our lives, as we start to build our character, these elements play a crucial role. Siblings are often our first friends, teaching us how to share, get along, and understand others' feelings. Playgrounds and classrooms are places where we learn how to make friends, handle disagreements, and figure out who we are in a larger group.

The initial encounters of our lives leave lasting marks on how we think, feel, and act. It does not matter whether we grow up with a lot of advantages or suffer from scarcity; whatever we deal with, it shapes how we see and perceive the world around us, and it truly reflects in our decisions. There is one thing very interesting about human behavior: the way people interact with us. It guides us to how we feel about ourselves, and consequently, it adds to our confidence as well. Positive interactions directly contribute to our self-esteem and self-confidence, while negative encounters may lead to self-doubt and insecurity.

How we handle our relationships, feelings, and their expressions, our connections, and how we cater to them are all also linked with our early age events. It also teaches us how to face challenges, adapt to changes, and stay strong when things get tough. Sometimes, it feels surreal that a lot was happening in our childhood, but we did not notice it. Actually, that age was setting the stage for us to perform in the later years. It exactly acts as the platform on which we now accomplish our goals.

Just like all, even in my memory, my childhood is safe, serving as a guiding torch, allowing me to make decisions, enjoy new adventures, and adapt to new things as they happen. My identity was built within my family, and my parents had a huge impact on me and on my personality. The way they treated me eventually became the core of who I am today. I must say they both had a unique combination of personalities, and that was because of their personal experiences. Among many things that left a permanent mark on my personality, my parents are, for sure, one of them.

In my family's history, if someone stands out, it is my paternal grandfather. To give you a glimpse, you all must have heard of the American Dream, but he had lived it. He came from a family of ten children, and his identity was deeply tied to Jewish traditions. My great-grandfather was a well-respected Rabbi in Russia. Through this strong connection our family had a strong sense of faith and spirituality.

My grandfather's journey took a different path. A difficult one indeed. He had to leave the school after eighth grade, and all his learning was from the real-life experiences he encountered in life. In the beginning, he was a determined person, so he decided to become an entrepreneur and started from scratch. Through continuous hard work and constant struggle here and there, he then built a multimillion-dollar company that provided uniforms to the US Army. His persistent hard work proved that you can be successful despite not having much of a formal education. Your education cannot limit your potential to achieve your goals; it just resides within yourself, and through resilience, you can achieve it.

My grandmother was a different personality altogether, and the turning point in their story came from my grandmother's desire to travel and see the world beyond their home in Brooklyn. She wanted to experience new adventures in her life. And there, my grandfather never stopped her from dreaming; in fact, he made a tough choice out of sheer love for her, and he sold his company. He gave up the chance to benefit from it just before World War II. We all know how much more money he could have made if he had run the company during the war. Still, even without that potential wealth, he created a good life for himself and his family.

With his dedicated nature and constant hard work, my grandfather changed not only his life but also all the people around him. He had a beautiful house in Brooklyn, exactly as dreamt by my grandmother. She wanted to live in the lively spirit of the city. They enjoyed a life filled with luxuries, providing comfort for their growing family. It was these fulfilling times when my father was born. He grew up surrounded by elegance and privilege.

I am truly fortunate that I was born into such a brilliant family that valued knowledge and wisdom. When I was growing up, my father was the biggest influence on me; he had an extraordinary IQ of 165. I was inspired by his brilliance.

It was obvious that a person with such a high IQ could not go unnoticed, and rightly so; he achieved academic success early in his life. He was just 14 years old when he started college at Columbia University. He was very studious since the beginning. All his teachers and class fellows acknowledged his brilliance.

During his studies, my father discovered his passion for pursuing the law. He then worked hard to understand the legal field, sharpening his skills in persuasion and critical thinking. Even in law school, his genius mind helped him create strong and lasting impressions on qualified and senior lawyers.

Later on, when World War II loomed on the horizon, it drew my father into a different service. He joined the US Army, and his radiant mind was perfect for the intelligence unit of the army. He made critical war strategies, and with great bravery, he helped preserve freedom and played an important role in liberating Luxembourg. The senior army officers recognized his courageous efforts, and he was awarded a prestigious honor similar to being knighted.

My mother was a woman of grace and elegance. She was born in a special place where her Jewish heritage gets mixed with Southern traditions. With all its charm and history, Atlanta became her hometown. In the neighborhood, Jewish families were not very common, so my mother was a symbol of diversity, which made our world richer.

My mother's last name was Smullyan, taken after my grandfather when he left Russia and arrived at Ellis Island before moving to Atlanta. The influences of Jewish culture blended with the lively Southern atmosphere, shaping her identity through faith, community, and rich Southern culture.

Later, a big change happened; my grandfather's business required him to be in New York, so we decided to move to New York. There, my mother attended her high school, and after high school, she became a model, she was attracted by the city's busy pulse and all the opportunities that awaited her there.

For my mother, New York was just more than a high school; since the beginning, she has believed in the opportunities that lay there. One interesting incident happened when a producer was struck by her beauty and offered her to fly to Hollywood for a screen test. He even suggested a stage name for her if she thought to accept that.

Well, fate had it the other way; before she could make any decision, her father stepped in. He was a conservative man, and he had a lot of concerns about her working in Hollywood. To him, the movie stars were morally questionable, and he eventually suggested she stay back in New York.

While my mother was modeling, an incident happened that totally changed the course of her life. She crossed paths with my father, and little did they know, they both met with each other's soul mates. As they connected, the sparks of attraction ignited, and a love story began, set against the vibrant backdrop of New York City.

With all her heart, my mother respected her father's wishes and completely ignored the idea of going to Hollywood and accepted her destiny with my father. Their marriage marked the start of a new chapter filled with love, shared dreams, and the promise of a life together.

In the glamorous circles of New York's elite, my parents moved through a world full of sophistication and privilege. They mingled with Broadway actors and Cafe Society, living in a place where dreams came true and ambitions soared. This remarkable setting laid the groundwork for my own story.

My father came home, and we were living on the upper westside of Manhattan where I was born. As time passed, my parents, my sister, and I decided to start a new chapter. We left the lively city behind and moved to Long Island, looking for a quieter life and new opportunities in the suburbs.

Moving to Long Island was a big change for me as a 5-year-old child. It was a time when the suburbs represented success and a better life, a place where everybody was living a stable life. Surrounded by well-kept lawns. I began to see the world through the lens of a suburban life. It was simple, prosperous, and full of hopes and dreams.

My parents were loving and supportive. They always made sure my sister and I were fully cared for, both for material and emotional needs. Because of this, my tendency to please others didn't come from feeling neglected. Instead, it came from wanting to make them proud and not wanting to disappoint them in any way.

From a very young age, I learned the importance of being polite. Since, it started so early, now it is an integral part of my whole character. I chose my words carefully, knowing that saying anything offensive was not acceptable. These teachings shaped how I interacted with others and how I presented myself to the world.

Beneath the surface of a perfect family, my tendency to please others took root. Growing up in a home with accomplished people made me feel like I needed to prove my worth and seek approval from my family. My father always taught me that perfection and obedience are the keys to acceptance. My father was a strong man with high achievements and high expectations, and he hugely influenced me. Therefore, his words stuck with me, reminding me to stay in line, respect my boundaries, and always aim to make others happy.

These early experiences led to my need to please others becoming a big part of who I am. I became very aware of what people wanted and expected from me, often putting their needs before my own. This desire for approval turned into a strong drive that influenced my relationships and decisions as I grew up and faced the challenges of adulthood.

Chapter 2

Young love is a beautiful thing. It brings out the best of us as it is filled with joy, vulnerability and new experiences. It is a romantic thing that comes straight out of our hearts. It helps us figure out what we want in a partner and what kind of person fits well with us. When we first fall in love, we do so with innocent hearts, not fully understanding how much it will shape our future.

Love teaches us in a very unnoticed manner. It takes us to the highs and lows of life to let us know that there is a lot to life, just more than being an ordinary person. We begin to see that shared values, good communication, and respect are key to building a strong connection.

It allows us to reveal our true selves to the people we passionately connect with and feel the warmth of it. We feel safe enough to share our dreams and fears because we know that we are fully understood now.

However, it also comes with its own set of challenges. It pushes us to grow and learn about the boundaries we need to maintain our identity. We work to find the right balance between loving someone fully and staying true to ourselves. When we face heartbreak, we find the strength to let go of relationships that aren't right for us. In doing so, we cement our self-worth and recognize that not every connection is meant to last.

When we come out of young love, we are more self-aware and have a clearer sense of what we certainly need in our lives. We come across a realization that love isn't just about big gestures or fleeting feelings but about empathy, trust, and emotional support that partners give to each other. It becomes the stepping stone to experience something mature, which has true connectivity and a deeper connection.

As it was not a common discussion in my household, the subject of "sex" has always made me uncomfortable. So much so that I was called "Prudent" in my high school. To be honest, I wasn't either so much interested in it. My whole sole focus was on the fashion industry. Well, things changed when I met my first boyfriend in my senior year. He was in another high school, and the moment we met, we were together every day, then, in the following year, he attended the prestigious Walton School at Penn, and we had fell in love with each other.

For two and a half years, we were inseparable. In my junior year of high school, I applied at the University of Cincinnati, long before I met the first love of my life. I felt conflicted because I had applied, and I knew that I had to leave. Our senior year was emotional; we spent nearly all the time together. I adored him, and he loved me with all his heart.

When I saw him for the first time, my heart was filled with excitement. His personality was charming, which immediately drew me in. His eyes were deep and warm, which made me feel at ease as if we were meant to meet.

As time passed, our connection grew stronger. We used to talk for countless hours, discussing our dreams, hopes, fears, and everything else under the sun. To me, his words were quite comforting, and they used to bring me great joy. The more we used to talk, my feelings for him deepened, and eventually, I found myself falling in love with him.

However, there was one challenge: beneath our fairytale relationship, I started noticing his controlling side.

He was really possessive and demanding, though, at that time, I hesitated to acknowledge it. Still, I held onto our love, hoping that with time, he would learn to trust me more.

Looking back, those days were like an emotional roller coaster. There was excitement of the young love, the fear of dependency, and uncertainty about the future. Despite all the challenges, I convinced myself that our love would surely overcome anything. Even with his controlling nature, I believed love would prevail.

Me at my college graduation

When I started at the University of Cincinnati, the distance between us began to take a toll. The frequent flights to see him only made the separation harder. Eventually, I realized I needed to be closer to him. So, I decided to transfer back home to Adelphi on Long Island, wondering now if it was the right choice. The things we do for love.

At Adelphi, I pursued my passion for psychology, eager to understand the human mind and behavior. Alongside my studies, I found comfort in fine arts, using painting to express the emotions I carried within. My dedication paid off, and I earned straight A's for four years.

I also started dancing and acting because they both helped me express my emotions, which I was unable to express through my words. Through dance, I was expressing myself with the help of movements, and of course, acting was helping me bring life to the characters, for which I was drawing inspiration from psychology studies. Well, these creative pursuits helped me later in my life.

As time went on, our relationship began to change. Mark, the man I thought I knew, changed in ways I hadn't expected. The distance and years apart altered him, and our once-strong connection started to weaken. Well, I felt the pain, but I found strength by immersing myself in my psychology studies and using my artistic side for emotional relief.

Mark found success in Washington, D.C., after completing his graduation law degree, where he built a thriving law firm. Life's journey often leads us down different paths, and though we had grown apart, I held on to the wonderful memories we created together. I carried the growth I gained from our relationship into my future, where my love for psychology and the arts opened up new and fulfilling opportunities.

My break with Mark was painful. Well, as soon as I healed from it, I made myself busy in the lively atmosphere of sorority life at Adelphi. Here, another romantic chapter of my life was waiting for me. I met Jared, the brother of my sorority sisters. This man profoundly impacted my life.

Jared had a captivating charm and charisma that drew me in. Although I didn't feel an instant physical attraction, I quickly realized that his inner qualities were far more impressive. His kindness, humor, and magnetic personality cast a spell on my heart, revealing a depth that was truly remarkable.

With each date we shared, Jared had a special talent for creating unforgettable experiences, from amazing nights at Carnegie Hall, where the music lifted our spirits, to candlelit dinners at graceful restaurants that delighted our senses. He definitely added a magic touch to my life. It wasn't just about the places we went; it was his attention to detail that made every moment joyful.

In his company, my heart bloomed like a flower, and laughter became the soundtrack of our lives. There was a sense of ease and comfort between us as if we were two souls in perfect harmony. While physical attraction wasn't the main focus, our deeper connection brought me great happiness.

As my relationship with Jared was getting stable, I realized that love can take many forms. It doesn't always have to be intense; sometimes, it can be gentle, just like a delicate flower releasing its sweet scent. Jared showed me the beauty of emotional connections and the joy of shared moments. He taught me that love can emerge from unexpected places and that true happiness lies in appreciating the uniqueness of every relationship that comes into our lives.

During our time together, Jared openly expressed his deep desire to make me his life partner. He proposed to me five times, with each request more sincere than the last. However, at just around 20 years old, I felt too young to accept his heartfelt offers. I knew in my heart that I needed more time to experience life fully before making such a big commitment.

I clearly remember it was one cold night, the snowflakes twirled under the soft glow of Central Park's streetlights, and Jared's love reached a peak. In a romantic horse-drawn carriage, he nervously asked me once again to marry him. My heart ached as I looked into his sincere eyes, knowing I cared for him deeply but still wasn't ready for marriage. I gently turned him down once more, and in that bittersweet moment, we both understood it was time to go our separate ways.

Life took us down different paths, and Jared found success in the media industry. He achieved great things at ABC and eventually became the executive vice president of ESPN. My admiration for his accomplishments only grew over the years. After retiring, the Federal Communications Commission (FCC) even sought his advice as a consultant.

Although our romance didn't change the course of my life, but still Jared left a lasting mark on my heart. The laughter, shared moments, and genuine affection became fond memories that I still treasure. Though we parted ways, the bond we built during that time remained special.

At 21, I began the journey of my own independence. Graduation marked the end of college and the start of a new chapter filled with possibilities. Though Jared and I had moved on, I carried the lessons and warmth of our love with gratitude, knowing he helped shape the person I was becoming as I stepped into adulthood.

Chapter 3

A short while after my graduation, I started searching for a job and luckily found one at Business Week Magazine. I was truly excited because of the financial independence it would come along with and also that it would be my first professional mark in the world.

I was in the commercial department because, at the time, I was undecided about where I wanted to be in life and what I wanted to do in the future. Pursue my master's? Get a job related to either of my two degrees? And in that case, which one would I pursue, a career in psychology or fine arts? Or should I go to fashion school like I'd originally wanted to? I was unsure; therefore, to think more appropriately and to organically reach the decision, I gave myself time by doing neither of them. But I also don't want to sit idle so I had to get the job.

I learned the ropes pretty quickly and was an efficient worker in no time. I was a diligent employee who always tried to outdo myself and do better each time, and I was well-liked around the office. Soon, I'd made plenty of friends around the place, and I was enjoying my life greatly. Though I had real responsibilities to manage, I felt unfulfilled.

I was also single. After Jared, I had boyfriends, mostly at summer camps, but none of them made me really feel something. They were almost like friends but with the boyfriend logo, but the only relationship-worthy thing we did was go out on dates but sex was always off the table. So, I had been in relationships but had not been involved in a serious one, and as of then, I was not too interested in the prospect of finding one, either. I felt like I had my whole life ahead of me, so I wasn't in a hurry to find a partner. I believed that when it was the right time, love would find me on its own.

Little did I know that it was going to be pretty soon.

I had a coworker at the magazine who was a married woman. She was very happy in her marriage, and she wanted me to find someone, too. She never pressured me about it or anything like that; she would just casually try to set me up with guys she thought were a good match. One day, she came into the office and told me that she had found someone she thought would be my type and that we were going to go out on a blind date. Since I had a free schedule on the day of the dinner, I agreed, mostly just to stop her from bugging me anymore.

She spent the whole day going on about how much I'd like this guy, and I'll admit, it got me curious, too. She couldn't show me his picture or anything like that, so I had to use my imagination only, and I had no choice but to wait until dinner to find out what this guy was like.

The day came, and I came home from work to dress up for the date. I might not have been keen on wanting to find someone for myself, but you never know what experience might lead you to a new phase of your life, and first impression matters a lot. I grew up in a family that was part of New York City's elite social circle, so dressing up for every occasion was something I learned early on. It was practically second nature to me. Since I also wanted to work in the fashion industry someday, therefore, finding the perfect outfit for any event was always an exciting task for me. It's just that picking out a dress brought me real joy.

I spent the evening getting ready for the date, making sure everything was perfect. The time we agreed on for him to pick me up finally arrived. Just as the hour struck, the doorbell rang right on time. It couldn't have been more perfectly timed. It was already a signal to me. Well, intrigued and slightly impressed by his punctuality because it was the bare minimum, and we still had the whole date remaining, I headed out of my room, down the staircase, and opened the door of the house for him. I was not prepared for the sight that greeted me or the feelings it sparked.

Then I invited him in, and he met my parents. Then we walked down the driveway to his car. He opened the car door for me.

Zac, the guy my coworker had spent the entire day talking about, was indeed a sight to see. The years may have faded my memory of his face, but I'll never forget how his eyes changed. Moments before, they seemed dull, but now they were gleaming, locked onto mine as if they were looking straight into my soul. He was a decent bit taller than me and had an air of intelligence about him. By looking at him, I just knew I was going to have a wonderful time on the date.

When we arrived at the restaurant where Zac had made reservations, I was struck by the ambiance of the place. As he checked in at the reception, I couldn't help but admire the surroundings. The waitress led us to our table by the window, and I loved the location. It was perfectly positioned — not too close to the band playing, but still close enough to feel the music's charm. This way, we could talk comfortably without raising our voices.

Once we ordered our food, the date began, and I realized my prediction was exactly spot on; it was going well. I reluctantly admitted to myself that my coworker had been right, too. We talked about everything under the sun, and I never once felt like our different professions or the fact that we didn't know each other before the date was a problem at all. The conversation flowed effortlessly over glasses of wine, making it easy to connect. Honestly, it was one of the best dates I had experienced up to that point.

The food turned out to be excellent, but the highlight of the evening was certainly the handsome gentleman sitting in front of me. Did I mention he opened the car door for me and also pulled out the chair for me? Small things like that had always mattered to me, things that I had always seen my father do for my mother without a second thought. Things that showed that the other person cared or that, at the very least, they were well-mannered because I supposed a first date is too soon to be thinking about if the other person likes you.

But the way everything was going, I was certain Zac was definitely interested in me; it was clear as day on his face. We had a lovely time together, and soon, it was time to head home.

Even after spending the whole date talking to each other, I was surprised to find that I wanted to keep talking to him. So I did, and we spent the whole car ride back to my home conversing. I was so caught up in our conversation that I didn't notice when he came to a sudden yet smooth stop. I was surprised to realize that we were already at my place.

In the time that I took to process this, he got out of the car and came over to my side to open the car door for me. I got out and suddenly felt rather shy, not knowing what to say. Maybe he caught on that I was feeling timid, so he held my hand in his own, firmly yet loosely, so that I could take it out of his grasp if I wanted to. I didn't.

In a soft, low voice, he whispered, "Did you enjoy the dinner?" He had a confident expression that said that he already knew my answer; his eyes displayed his nervous anticipation. I decided to put him at ease.

"I did," I replied in an equally low-pitched voice, and his body seemed to relax a little. He bent his head down, and I thought he was going to kiss me. Before I had the time to panic, he brought my hand closer to his face and pressed his lips to my knuckles. I let out a quiet sigh of relief. As much as I had enjoyed the date, I wasn't quite ready for anything more just yet. He got into his car, mock-saluted me, and started up the engine. His car exited my driveway, and once the engine of the car got out of my earshot, the driveway felt eerily silent.

It was in the silence of my driveway that I realized we had developed a slight crush on each other.

Our romance took flight. In the blink of an eye, me and Zac were caught up in love that was destined for both of us. Days turned into weeks and weeks into months as we enjoyed each other's company and discovered new sides of our personalities. Each date was filled with affection and meaningful conversations. These moments helped us grow closer. It felt like we were building something beautiful with every shared experience.

As time passed and our love grew, we both knew that we had got something truly special. It feels as if the universe has conspired to bring us together, and we didn't have any choice but to draw ourselves into it. It wasn't long before Zac got down on one knee, his eyes done shimmering with love and devotion, and he asked me to be his forever. Without a second thought coming to my mind, I wiped my tears of joy and excitement; I accepted his heartfelt proposal. In my heart, I knew that this was the man I wanted to spend the rest of my life with.

Three months after our unforgettable first date, we took a big step that would change our lives forever: getting engaged. It was a beautiful promise of a future full of love and commitment. This good news spread like wildfire in our friends' circle, and they all congratulated us with warm wishes.

Soon, we started planning our wedding, a celebration of our love that would reflect the true bond we had built together.

Four months after our engagement, we stood hand in hand, surrounded by a sea of loved ones, ready to take our vows. The air was filled with excitement as we became husband and wife, and it felt like that time was stopped. It was a magical moment, like a fairytale coming to life. When Zac looked at me and said, "I do," I felt a rush of gratitude and happiness filled my heart.

As husband and wife, we started a new chapter of our lives. We decided to create a home that would be a safe haven for our love. We chose to buy an apartment near the neighborhood where I grew up. The familiar streets were filled with happy memories, and being close to my past felt like the perfect way to begin our journey together as a married couple.

With each step we took, we built a love story that would last forever. Our apartment used to be the place where we shaped our dreams and hopes, filling it with treasured memories. Each day was filled with love and affection.

And so, the romance that started with a simple blind date blossomed into a lifetime filled with love, laughter, and shared dreams. As we strolled hand in hand through the streets rich with our memories, we were accepting our future with open arms. We realized that our love story was just the beginning of a wonderful tale that speaks of two souls united in love, destined to last a lifetime and beyond.

Me as a new mother

It wasn't easy to have a baby. We had been trying for a while, but it turned out that I had fertility issues. I had to go to a fertility doctor and go through two rounds of oral medication that didn't work and then two rounds of injections that finally were a success. Unfortunately, I developed an ovarian cyst the size of a grapefruit that left me in excruciating pain.

My doctor ordered me to take two weeks of bed rest to prevent the risk of it rupturing, which could have been life-threatening. It was a tough time, but I knew I had to prioritize my health.

But all that pain was worth it. With every heartbeat, I felt the precious life growing inside me, and each gentle kick reminded me of the miracle happening within. Nine months of waiting, nurturing, and awe led to a moment that would change our lives forever. As the sun set and the world quieted down, the moment we had been looking forward to finally arrived.

With mixed emotional feelings and quiet prayers, we welcomed our beautiful daughter into this world. I felt like the air around me stopped as she took her first breath, and everything seemed to be paused for a moment to celebrate her arrival. As her tiny fingers curled around mine, I knew that my heart would never be the same again.

Her birth was a reflection of the love between me and Zac. As we looked into her bright, curious eyes, we realized that we had gained a new purpose in life. With every soft touch and kind word, we made sure to be her source of strength and her steady support.

As time went on, our lives took unexpected turns that brought both joy and challenges. Zac's parents, who owned a successful packaging business, decided to move to a place in New Jersey. The place was close enough to Manhattan, but still not like before. While it was an exciting opportunity for Zac's family, it left me with mixed emotions and a lot of uncertainty.

As someone who has been a people pleaser, I didn't resist and went along. I left my life behind, saying goodbye to my family and friends to start this new adventure. I made this choice out of love for my husband and the hope of new opportunities.

Since the beginning, the idea of moving out to a new place was rather intimidating than exciting, especially with a new born baby. Still, we set out for this new chapter of life. The journey ahead was uncertain to me, but I knew that Zac and I would face it together, hand in hand, with determination and hope.

Shifting to a new place brought nostalgia for the home we had left behind. We exchanged the familiar sights with new ones as the busy city of Manhattan called us for more opportunities and dreams to pursue.

Although I was excited, deep down inside me, there was loneliness and vulnerability. I was hiding it. To be in the new place surrounded by Zac's family made me struggle with feelings of isolation. I missed my place, the familiar faces, and the comforting sense of home.

Getting used to this new part of my life while taking care of a newborn daughter was extremely challenging. I was already coping with being a first-time mother but without my family around made it harder. I often felt the weight of being a mom pressing down on me, and there were many moments when I found myself feeling doubtful about everything.

During the same time, my relationship with Zac started to go downhill. I found myself just going along with what he wanted, putting aside my own dreams and desires just to keep the peace. Even though I knew deep down that this wasn't how a healthy relationship should work, I kept falling into the same pattern. I just hoped that our love would be strong enough to overcome his controlling behavior.

Zac was always a big part of my life, but he too had the same controlling nature life many of my previous boyfriends, except Jared. He was different and always treated me like I was special. I was upset to see Zac's controlling behavior repeating again and again, and it created a lot more issues in our marriage. I started to feel like I was losing my independence and even my sense of self. And all of this was putting out the spark in our love.

During all these challenges, I really struggled with my feelings. I was caught between my love for Zac and my need to be my own person. Our love was real and genuine, but it felt overshadowed by his controlling nature. I kept reminding myself that love should be about freedom and understanding, not something that feels like a heavy weight holding me down. On top of that, there was no communication, and misunderstandings seemed to fill our days. I found myself missing those carefree moments when we would talk and laugh easily, just like we did on our early dates.

I finally decided it was time for a change. Something that could either revive our love or mark the end of our journey together. I'd thought long and hard about it, but I knew I had to suggest we see a marriage counselor. When I brought it up to Zac, I was pretty nervous about how he'd take it. Thankfully, he was open to the idea.

As we entered the counselor's office, I felt the heaviness. I was hopeful but nervous at the same time. As I started opening up about the issues in our relationship, I was really hopeful that the counselor could help us find our way back to the love we used to have.

But honestly, time had really worn me down, and the wounds that had been there for so long weren't going to heal overnight. The counselor offered some great advice and strategies, but it felt like the gap between us was too wide to bridge. I knew we had once shared something special, but those past struggles had left some deep scars.

So, while we were going through all this counseling, a new neighbor moved into our building, and it caught me off guard. The first time I bumped into him, I felt the spark I didn't even know was still there. I was attracted to his kindness, and there was just something about the way he understood me that felt refreshing.

As we kept going to counseling, things got really complicated. That interaction with the new neighbor made me confused between the feelings of love and friendship. Honestly, I didn't see that coming. Although the counselor was giving us great advice, my heart was not in the right place; it was tangled with a mess of emotions. I was stuck between the love I used to have with Zac and this new connection that felt really exciting but also confusing.

During this whole time, I realized that my relationship with Zac had reached a point of no return. The relationship was just wearing me down, and our differences felt huge. The counseling sessions helped me reflect a bit, but they also opened my eyes to something I couldn't ignore anymore: the love I once had for Zac had turned into something wistful.

Now, it was time to say goodbye and part ways.

Chapter 4

In the wide, hot desert, something strange often happens, a mirage. This is a trick that makes you see things that aren't really there. Under the blazing sun, when you're thirsty and tired, you might spot what looks like an oasis far away. It seems to be a place full of green plants and cool water, like a promise of relief.

Your heart fills with hope, and you think your long walk is finally over. But as you get closer, the oasis fades away, disappearing into the hot air. You're left standing in the empty desert with nothing but a feeling of disappointment. Even though people know it's just an illusion, a mirage still fools anyone who wants to believe it.

That's how my story with Max began. A story that feels a lot like a mirage. Max, fresh out of a divorce and without a job, seemed like a warning in himself. All the signs were there, bright as red flags, but there was something about him that pulled me in.

He moved through the dating world like it was no big deal, leaving his mark on many women in our building. I knew it was probably smarter to avoid someone like him, but I couldn't help myself. His charm drew me in.

In the middle of my everyday life, I crossed paths with Max. It felt like a simple meeting at first, but it soon became much more. From that day on, our lives started to connect, and our story began. It was filled with brief, shared looks, quick meetings in the hallway, and small talk. The more I got to know Max, the more I saw that he was a mix of mystery and warning signs.

His past was full of heartbreak and hard times, and his present was unclear, with no job and a lot of questions. Still, there was something about him that kept drawing me in, something that didn't make sense but was impossible to ignore. Something that defied my rationality completely.

Back then, my life was predictable and mundane, and in the middle of such mediocrity, the idea of Max stood out in my mind. He seemed to offer an escape from my usual schedule, from which I was definitely not happy.

Even though a part of me warned against falling for the charm, I couldn't help but feel pulled toward him. Maybe it was the excitement of stepping into something unexpected, of breaking away from the familiar path I'd always followed.

Max stirred up my feelings, but among all the emotions, one stood out, and that was curiosity. I really wanted to understand who he was because of his mannerisms; there were a lot of contrasts. However, our talks gave me little bits of his story, his thoughts, his past, and what kept him going. Each conversation was like a new page, showing me his hopes, his worries, and everything that made him who he was.

Even though, in hindsight, I knew better, I couldn't stop myself from thinking there could be something real between us, even if it didn't last. I felt a mix of excitement and warning. I knew the whole thing was not in my best interest, but I pursued it anyway.

However, the story still plays out, showing that the heart can be drawn in, even when we know something is not real. My first impression of Max is still clear in my mind. It's a reminder of how tricky human connections can be, a mix of curiosity and carefulness, and a balance between desire and knowing what's best.

Oh, I should back up and begin the story by telling you how we met.

Our apartment building had a shared pool that drew everyone in, especially on hot summer weekends. Most of our neighbors went there and spent time together, but Zac was the only man there. He used to sit by the pool, but he seemed out of place, like an island in the middle of all the fun and talking.

Even though Zac never used to hang out with us, I had no trouble making friends. I used to spend time at the poolside and meet with other neighbors. Nicole was a single mom with a young kid, and we really hit it off! We connected through our shared experiences and helped each other out. Honestly, I didn't realize it at the time, but our friendship would end up having a big impact on my life.

Actually, it was Nicole who introduced Max to me. It was because of her that our paths crossed. She had a real knack for making connections, and her friendship with Max started an unexpected journey for both of us. I had no idea back then that this introduction would lead to a big moment that would change my life in many ways.

Very soon, I found myself in long conversations with Max, and those conversations were flowing effortlessly. It was like we were discovering things we both understood. Even though we came from different backgrounds, we found common ground in what we thought and believed. Our talks showed a connection that went beyond the usual differences like religion, family, and social status. Instead of pulling us apart, those differences actually made our bond stronger because we both had unique views to share.

He was a lapsed Catholic, and I was a practicing Jew, but when we talked, our different religions didn't matter at all. He was in working-class traditions, while mine was more high-class. But when we chatted, those differences didn't mean much. It felt like we were connecting on a deeper level, building a strong friendship as we shared our thoughts.

Our dreams and how we used to perceive different things were the common points that connected us and brought us together. Each time we talked, we felt closer, and it didn't matter what society expected from us. It was like our souls had known each other before, as if we were reuniting after being apart for a long time. Being around each other made our differences turn into things that added to our friendship.

As time went on, our bond got stronger. Despite all our problems, there were waves of laughter and conversations happening between us. We discovered that real understanding goes beyond what people see on the outside.

It felt like our hearts and minds fit perfectly together, like two pieces of a puzzle. And before I knew it, I fell in love with him. Well, how could I not? He was such a romantic person back then. He would write songs for me and sing them on his guitar since he used to be the lead singer for a local band. We'd play Scrabble almost daily, and he would spell out "I love Brittany" on the board. He'd bring me flowers daily and cook for me, and there were other things like that that I found endearing and charming and attracted me to him.

I was suffering from homesickness due to having moved to New Jersey and was extremely vulnerable, and during that period of emotional turmoil, Max was my rock.

Max's unexpected intrusion into my thoughts and conversations caught me off guard. Nights were no longer silent; they were painted with his presence, each passing hour spent unraveling the threads of our conversations. Talking about Max with Nicole, someone I trusted, made me realize just how strong my feelings for him really were.

At first, I was denying my feelings, it felt safer that way. I know my emotions were confusing me, and I didn't want to face them. The idea that I, a married woman, was getting caught up in feelings for someone who wasn't my husband felt strange and uncomfortable. I could hear society's expectations in my head, making it even harder to deal with what I was feeling.

But I couldn't ignore my heart anymore. I really had to face the truth I had been avoiding. It slowly became clear to me, like opening a dusty old book I hadn't read in years: the love that used to be the strong base of my marriage had faded away, leaving just a faint memory of it. The bond that once kept me steady now felt empty and hollow, like a shell of what it used to be. It was a hard pill to swallow, realizing how much things had changed.

The counseling sessions felt like a brief break, a little spark of hope that we could fix our relationship. But deep down, I knew things were too broken to fix. The sacrifices I made had worn away what we once had, leaving behind a dry, empty space where love used to grow.

I had lots of reasons to hold back from trying to save a connection that had fallen apart. The constant power struggles, the way my dreams were pushed aside, and how I often felt ignored had all damaged what we once had. Inside, I felt a quiet longing for something more than the dull life I was living. I wanted more than just getting by.

Deep down in my heart, I knew that my feelings for Max were more than a mere crush. To me, they were the promise of understanding, friendship, and support without any pressure. The idea of a connection that could lift me up instead of dragging me down was so tempting and hard to resist.

With each passing day, it became clearer to me that my marriage was stuck in a mundane routine and there was no spark left in it, and above all, this should not describe my life anymore. In front of me, there was a choice, one that didn't follow what society expected. I could see a future where I could reshape my life, where love could be real and fresh again.

Zac was very controlling. Not a little subtly controlling, but the kind that dictated what I wore and what I ate. Every Friday and Saturday, he had made this rule that we had to go out to eat, and it had to be the same two restaurants every week — one on Friday and another one on Saturday, but the same ones each week. There, he'd always order the same food and even order for me without asking what I wanted and if I wanted to order anything different.

Moreover, throughout three different points during the course of the meal, he would order drinks even though he was bad at handling his liquor. He was a mean drunk, and once under the influence, he would verbally abuse me. I was exhausted by his mannerisms and his promises of improving himself but never actually trying. We never had any verbal altercations; I would just sit and listen to him until I no longer could.

Moreover, the day after, he wouldn't remember his behavior from the night before and presume that everything was fine and we were good. He thought that we were going strong and looking to buy a house and expand our family, and I was the only one between the two of us who was bearing the weight of everything that was going wrong alone.

It wasn't me who first realized that his behavior was abusive; it was actually my sister and her friends. At parties, he would treat me like his maid. He would make sure that I would serve him the food; he would just basically treat me as a waitress.

My sister and friends observed this on multiple occasions and were surprised that I had never argued with him about it, but that was just who I was. A people pleaser who would do anything to make sure people were happy

So, once I realized that our marriage was not the way marriages were supposed to be and had also started developing feelings for Max, it was only a matter of time before I made a conclusive decision. Therefore, it was at the age of 28 that I decided to call it quits and end my seven-year-long marriage with Zac, a little sad but extremely delighted by the new beginning.

Chapter 5

The divorce left me drowning in deep emotional pain and devastation. Each day felt like a relentless battle against panic attacks that would tighten their grip on me, leaving me breathless and overwhelmed. Tears became my constant companion, silent evidence of the shattered dreams and the immense weight of heartbreak I carried. I was no longer the composed individual I once knew; I became an emotional wreck, lost in a sea of overwhelming feelings that felt like they might swallow me whole.

To make things worse, my ex-husband's financial support was barely enough, falling far short of what he should have been providing as the father of our child. As I had taken up the responsibility of being a housewife for the duration of our seven-year-long marriage, I lacked the relevant experience that would help me get a job that paid adequately, let alone handsomely. The monthly stipend he provided was a trivial sum, leaving us shaking on the brink of financial instability.

Consequently, at the start of each month, a sense of fear would settle over me, knowing that I would have to approach my father to ask for financial assistance. He never made me feel bad about it; on the contrary, he was my rock throughout the entire tumultuous experience. Even then, it was a humbling experience, one that left me grappling with a sense of inadequacy and dependency.

Gratefully, my father extended his helping hand, offering the financial support we needed to make ends meet. I always did my best to repay every penny he had lent me, determined not to let the burden weigh heavily on him.

However, over time, a growing resolve took root within me. I could no longer bear the thought of becoming a constant source of financial strain on my father's shoulders. I made the difficult choice to turn down any more help, deciding to find my own way through the tough situation.

While my mother, in her own enigmatic way, stood by my side, her actions spoke a different tale. We'd walk through the store together, but she only bought things for herself, never for me or my daughter, even though she knew we were struggling financially. It seemed like she didn't fully understand how hard things were for us, as her focus remained on her own wants. It was a painful example of how love and understanding can sometimes be lost in the midst of personal emotions. I did not hold it against her—it was nice that she drove all the way to be with me each week, but her lack of thoughtfulness impacted me emotionally due to the vulnerable state of mind that I was in.

My father's perception and generosity, in stark contrast to my mother's actions, did not go unnoticed. He recognized the evident gap between my mother's efforts and the support I needed. In a quiet gesture of kindness, he offered his help, giving us the means to ease our struggles. With a gentle push, he encouraged her to buy two outfits for me, showing his silent support and deep love.

I wore one of those outfits on two different occasions, one day filled with memories and the other with questions about the future. It was the same outfit I chose for the courtroom, where I faced the reality of ending a chapter of my life that had been entwined with Zac's, and it was also the same outfit I had worn on my wedding day with Max, a day that once held promises of forever. The fabric told the story of life's ups and downs, its threads connecting moments of love, loss, and the strong bond between a father and his daughter.

***

The ripples of the divorce extended far beyond my own heartache, affecting the life of my daughter, Alice, who was two-and-a-half years old at the time of our separation and four at the time of our divorce, in profound ways. The separation brought a painful reality, taking away her innocence and changing how she saw the world.

Things didn't get any better for her afterward, either. I tried to be everything for her: a mother, father, and friend. Not that I wasn't already since her father was an old-fashioned man. In the way that he didn't believe he was ever wrong or that anything was even remotely his fault, he also believed raising the children was the mother's job and, therefore, had never helped me with anything when it came to Alice. But I obviously could not fill the void left by her father's absence.

Sometime after our divorce, my ex-husband chose to get married to another woman. His decision to remarry introduced a new dynamic that further distanced him from the responsibility he held as a father. The woman he chose to wed had a son from a previous marriage, and a little while after the wedding, they had a child of their own, too. In this new family dynamic, the attention seemed to shift, leaving my daughter feeling distant from her father's love.

With the birth of their child, a new chapter seemed to unfold, one that did not include Alice in the narrative of their family. The woman's attitude made my daughter feel left out, leaving her longing for the attention and love she deserved. The shifts were palpable, a cruel reminder of the emotional absence that began to define her relationship with her father.

The journey from being a cherished daughter to an occasionally visited child was a painful one. There was a time when my ex-husband fought to spend weekends and holidays with her, but over time, it faded into short visits on random Sundays. Her birthdays were marked by the evident absence of the one who had helped to bring her into this world.

The transformation was not only in his physical presence but also in his emotional availability. The closeness that once defined their relationship became a distant memory. It was replaced by a growing gap, leaving Alice wanting a connection that seemed to slip further away.

The emotional turmoil that followed deeply affected Alice's early years. The problems in their relationship grew wider, and occasional verbal abuse made the pain even worse. The absence of a loving father figure became a haunting presence in her life, manifesting itself in the form of behavioral issues when she was in high school, even though it was years after our divorce.

As we worked through these challenges, trying to help Alice navigate high school, the suggestion of a boarding school came up. It was a decision we reached with a heavy heart, driven by the desire to provide her with the support she needed. However, it came at a price—the necessity for her to be separated from the environment that was familiar to her. She was recommended not to return to my house for the summer and other holidays.

As if the thought of rarely seeing her wasn't hard enough, the decision was met with resistance from my ex-husband. He refused to take her in for the summer, fearing it would "spoil" his own children's time, showing just how emotionally distant he had become.

It was a harsh truth that shattered any remaining hope that he truly cared about his daughter's well-being. Imagine being a teenager in her formative years, being told to keep a distance from her mother's house, and being rejected by her own father. It brings me to tears, thinking about all those summers that she had to stay back at the facility, accompanied by only a few teachers and what was probably a profound sense of loneliness.

The day he placed her on a train back to the facility was a heartrending moment that etched itself into Alice's memory. She felt abandoned and deserted, a betrayal that wounded her spirit and left her grappling with a pain that defied words. Her heartache was something she felt deeply, a burden she carried with her as she returned to the boarding school, the place where she found comfort and safety.

As the years passed, the echoes of her past continued to ring in her life. The absence of a strong male role model casts a long shadow, leaving her struggling to form healthy relationships with men to this day. The scars of her early experiences shaped her perspective, influencing her interactions and choices in ways she sometimes struggled to understand.

***

As the days turned into months, the prospect of a wedding ceremony began to take shape. November brought with it the whisper of new beginnings, and among the fall foliage, Max and I made a decision that would mark the next chapter of our love story. We had planned to celebrate our union with an outdoor luncheon at The Tavern on the Green in Central Park, surrounded by its charming atmosphere, in June of the following year. At least, that was the plan.

I can still feel the excitement that pulsed through my veins as my mother and I sat down for lunch at the very place that would become a canvas for our joyous occasion. The clinking of glasses and the laughter that danced through the air seemed to infuse the very atmosphere with a sense of anticipation. We decided to put down a deposit for the wedding.

After our meal, we made our way to my father's office, with the city's buzz filling the air around us. Riding the elevator, I felt a wave of familiarity, recalling all the times I had taken this same ride. Soon, I was standing outside his office.

To this day, I vividly remember the entire scene that led up to the moment that changed my life. My father was yelling at a junior partner in his firm. I was waiting for him to finish their discussion so that we could go downstairs, where my mother was waiting for us. In the meantime, the entire office, which knew that I had recently gotten engaged, buzzed with congratulations and warm wishes, a chorus of voices that embraced me in a cocoon of happiness.

In that moment, as emotions surrounded me, I felt a deep sense of peace. It was as if things were finally falling into place, bringing a sense of harmony that had been missing for so long. The journey had been filled with challenges and heartache, but in that office, surrounded by the well-wishes of colleagues and my father's pride, I knew I had found a place of love and happiness.

Still reveling in the warmth of well-wishes and the echoes of laughter, my father and I stepped into the corridor. As the elevator doors opened, my father and I stepped into the elevator, and everything changed in an instant. Before I could fully process it, my father collapsed into my arms in that heart-stopping moment; I realized just how fragile and unpredictable life can be.

My heart raced, and a heart-wrenching scream tore through my throat as I held him, desperate for help that seemed agonizingly out of reach.

The superintendent heard me crying and yelling and was summoned to aid in the crisis that had shattered our world. I pleaded for him to fetch my mother, who waited in the Cadillac parked outside. Every second felt like it stretched on forever, a harsh reminder of just how fragile life can be. An ambulance arrived, its siren slicing through the air, yet the seconds stretched on, elongating into an agonizing stretch of uncertainty. As the EMTs worked to revive my father, my legs shook, showing just how deeply I was in shock. My mother and I huddled on the stairs, our eyes fixed on the scene unfolding before us, a silent prayer on our lips.

An EMT approached, his words laden with finality, the weight of his question hanging heavily in the air. "Are you the family of the deceased?"

With one question, the heartbreaking truth settled in: my father was gone, leaving a void that could never be filled. The world seemed to freeze, a scene of shock and sorrow that felt impossible to grasp. There was nothing more that I could do than nod in affirmation and be left reeling from the news that my father, a man with a presence larger than life and the person who had been there for me during the worst times of my existence, was no longer among the living.

As the EMTs departed to retrieve a body bag, I found myself drawn to the elevator, a foolish impulse that led me to a haunting sight. There, propped against the cold metal walls, my father's eyes remained open, a silent testament to a moment frozen in time. The image would forever be etched in my memory, a visual scar that bore witness to the abrupt departure of a loved one.

After the shock and sorrow settled, the weight of responsibility hit me. I knew I had to contact Max, who was making his way through the busy streets of Manhattan. Practicality took precedence, and plans were set in motion to transfer my father's body to the city morgue. As a chapter of life closed on city property, a new chapter of grief and transition lay before us.

Through the tears and heartache, I packed a bag, my hands moving automatically as I gathered what I needed. The journey to Long Island, where my mother sought solace, felt both surreal and necessary since I didn't want her to be alone after my dad's passing. I had made arrangements to leave my daughter with a trusted babysitter, not wanting to expose her to the grieving environment of my parents' house and remove her from familiar surroundings. I left the comfort of home, stepping into a journey shaped by loss, change, and unknowns.

My father's passing at the relatively tender age of 63 became an indelible marker in the journey of my life. It was a seismic shift, a moment that forever altered the course of my existence. His absence felt even heavier with everything else: a recent divorce, a new relationship, and a lingering sense of feeling out of place. The threads of my narrative had been rewoven, leaving me to navigate the intricate terrain of grief, love, and a world forever transformed.

Chapter 6

My father's passing made our lives change forever.

While we were thinking it over, my lawyer shared some practical advice that made the decision more complicated. He looked at our situation from a legal point of view and pointed out the practical realities of our relationship. Sharing a home and a life, we had already built a foundation that merged our individual worlds, which in turn lessened the rationale for delaying the marriage from a legal standpoint. According to him the best decision would be to get married as soon as possible, without any delay.

Another unexpected change was that Max went back on his promise to convert to Judaism. He admitted he had only agreed to it to win my father's approval. Now that was no longer a factor, he did not wish to convert and hoped that I would accept him for who he was. I accepted his change of mind, not knowing then what I know now about his habit of going back on his word. It was a very tough decision to make. Given the fact that my father had passed away very recently and the ache caused by his demise had yet to lessen, let alone subside altogether. I didn't want to agree to it. As we talked, balancing emotions and practical matters became very hard. Each perspective was important, and we had to find a way to respect the past while figuring out how to move forward.

Ultimately, the decision that emerged bore the weight of our collective aspirations and the practical realities that defined our journey. Despite the sadness we were facing, we decided to move forward with the wedding as a symbol of our love and commitment for the sake of legal requirements. It marked the start of a new chapter, showing how strong people can be even during hard times. The big day arrived for the second time in my life; unlike what we had planned, the ceremony did not take place in June but rather in March. The simplistic ceremony took place at my apartment, where I had made hors d'oeuvres for the occasion and had chosen my lovely daughter to be our flower girl. This time, there were no butterflies or nervous anticipation—there was little that could've gone wrong. There was a simple, heartfelt atmosphere filled with love, completely different from the lavishness of my first wedding. Surrounded by the presence of our closest friends and family, the atmosphere felt intimate—each person present was a cherished part of our shared journey. As I stood there, I felt both happy and reflective, thinking about the past. The dress I wore was special to me because it reminded me of both the good and the difficult moments I had experienced along the way. It was the very dress my father had gently persuaded my mother to buy, a gesture that now tugged at my heartstrings in ways I could never have anticipated. I felt the emptiness of his absence deeply. His memory seemed to linger like a quiet whisper in the air.

As the evening went on, I couldn't stop feeling the pain of missing my father. His absence was always in my mind, and I couldn't shake the emptiness it left. Yet, as I looked around at the faces of those who stood beside us, I realized that his spirit was very much present. The memory of his love and support had shaped me into the person I am today, and though he wasn't physically here, his legacy lived on in every moment that I shared with those I held dear.

As the event went on, I felt both the past and the future come together. The wedding that had gone wrong was now a memory, replaced by the calm of the present moment. The promises we made to each other brought our stories together, creating something special and unique to us. The day went smoothly, showing how love and simple celebrations can be beautiful. After we said our vows and became a couple, everyone went to a local Italian restaurant to enjoy a meal and celebrate the happy occasion.

In the wake of our marriage, the merging of our lives took on a new dimension as Max and I came back to my apartment where he was living for 7 months, and then everything started to feel different. We were excited about what the future would hold, but the weeks that followed brought lessons about trust and what it really means to be in a partnership. I watched Max remove the custom furniture that had been in my apartment, and I couldn't believe it. He said it didn't match his style, and it felt like someone was ruining a beautiful song.

During this time, the memory of my father's passing felt strong. Max told me he wanted to invest $40,000 from my father's inheritance into a business, and he took that money from my mother and hired a decorator. He said when we sold our apartment, and would share, promising to give some of the profits to my mother as a kind gesture, which he never did, and he never invested the money in any business. He spoke about the future with hopes of success and growth.

As time went on, the promises started to fall apart. The truth came out, and I learned that everything Max had said was a lie. The story about the co-op he had told my mother was fake, meant to cover up the real situation. The inheritance he was supposed to invest had vanished, taken by his false intentions. Max's actions became harder to ignore. He secretly took the diamond engagement ring from my first marriage 2.5-carat diamond, a symbol of my past, and sold it. What used to be a meaningful reminder of a special time was now just money. He sold the ring at the ring repair store owned by his mother.

In the middle of the chaos, the trust we once had seemed completely broken. The lies that came out were nothing like the partnership we had promised with each other. The more I tried to understand what he had done, the more I realized the life we had planned was falling apart. And all our shared dreams were replaced by stories of lies and betrayal.

The impact of these truths changed our relationship forever, making me question what trust really meant. What had once seemed like a bright future was now filled with hurtful actions, showing me that even close relationships can have their dark sides. From the start, our marriage didn't feel like a love story. It wasn't built on mutual understanding or affection. Instead, it felt like I had to follow his every wish. Love, it seemed, only existed if I met his expectations, leaving little room for me to be myself.

His relationship with Alice, my four-year-old daughter at the time of our marriage, was full of tension that still exists today. There was an unspoken rivalry between them, and the words "I love you" to her by him were never said or shown. What should have been a loving bond turned into a silent competition filled with unsaid feelings and issues. As time went on, their relationship grew more and more difficult, turning into something much worse: an abusive atmosphere that affected all of us. I found myself caught in the middle, trying to fix the growing distance between them. They would argue, communication broke down, and I had to step in and try to make things better.

Looking back, I could see how much my own actions shaped everything that happened. I had this strong need to please others, and it became a problem. I often pushed aside my own needs just to keep things calm between us. I ended up being the one to try and fix their fights, all in an effort to hold onto a balance that was slowly slipping away.

It all started in a way that felt off, leading to a relationship that would turn into a long journey. This was no typical love story. Instead, it took me through challenges that made me question what I knew about relationships, strength, and the heart. With abuse and hidden feelings always in the background, I found myself on a path that would change me in ways I hadn't thought possible.

Chapter 7

Over the years, our relationship changed. The excitement and passion we once felt slowly faded away. Instead of feeling like a big, bright celebration, it became more like a small, flickering candle struggling to stay lit. What used to feel like a lively song now feels more like a quiet tune in the background, hard to notice with everything else going on in daily life. Max's attitude changed noticeably. It was like watching a sunny day gradually turn cloudy. Before marriage, it had seemed as if there was nothing and no one. I suppose it was the thrill of the chase that had made me worth the effort. Once I was "his," there was no apparent need for him to keep doing all the romantic gestures that he used to do.

The warmth we once shared was gone. Now, we just lived alongside each other, feeling distant, like two people in separate worlds. The notion of "partnership" that marriage was supposed to embody felt like an outdated concept, a distant memory that had lost its relevance. Our commitment felt weaker over time as if it was gradually falling apart.

Gone were the days when his care had been a constant presence, a gentle force that had provided comfort and self-confidence. The person I once relied on for support seemed distant now, leaving me to handle life's problems on my own and raise my daughter by myself. It was as though a wall had been erected between us. I felt emotionally distant from everyone except my daughter. It was me and my full-time housekeeping duties keeping me busy. Our interactions were transactional; I paid her for her services, and in return, she provided the care and attention that Max had once offered. The irony was hard to ignore— our marriage, which was meant to be a partnership built on love, support, and trust, had evolved into a business arrangement. The distance between us felt too big to fix, and I didn't know how to make things better. I sometimes wish I could go back in time; I don't know if I would not have chosen him had I known how my life would be this difficult.

The housekeeper was a reminder of the care I missed, but she only did her job for the paycheck. It was very different from the loving gestures Max and I once shared. The house felt more like a bunch of rooms than a home filled with shared memories. It was indeed a bizarre and rough experience in which hollowness was the constant companion. I was the witness to our emotional disintegration. The passage of time has transformed our love story into something unrecognizable. As our lives moved forward, I felt like I didn't belong in my own home.

One day, a phone call from a friend suddenly interrupted my routine. On a call, I was informed that Max wanted to go to *Bora Bora*, a place he had always dreamed of visiting. I was surprised by how unexpected it was, and his wish stayed in my mind, making me feel unsure about everything and that moment pushed me more towards the confusion.

"Bora Bora?" I repeated, my voice tinged with a mixture of confusion and incredulity. The idea of taking a sudden trip to a distant place for 16 days seemed both exciting and a bit unsettling. It felt like a big change, something completely different from our usual routine. "When does he want to go?" I inquired, my mind racing to grasp the logistics of this sudden adventure. The friend's response came swift and unexpected, the words leaving me momentarily stunned.

"Tomorrow," he replied, as if it were the most natural thing in the world. The word "tomorrow" echoed in my mind, making me feel like I had to act quickly. Suddenly, I was faced with a decision that needed an immediate answer.

The next few hours were busy, filled with packing and getting things ready. As I folded clothes and gathered what he needed, since I was the one packing for him, I couldn't shake the strange feeling. I was packing Max's bag for a trip I wouldn't be going on. The suitcase was open in front of me, and I couldn't help but feel unsure about everything. as I packed his things to support his plan. Sixteen days, how long his trip would last, as he said there would be no phone and no contacts felt like a long time ahead. The idea of no contact was uncomfortable, reminding me of the emptiness his absence would bring. I had accepted it, but as the days went on, it started to bother me more.

What if I needed him? The question lingered in the back of my mind like a persistent whisper. The days ahead felt uncertain, full of unknown possibilities and challenges. What if a problem arose, an unexpected hurdle that required his presence or advice? The doubt was always with me, reminding me of the limits of our situation. Soon after Max's departure, once I had the household all to myself and could hear my thoughts, I found myself grappling with the reality of his absence. The house, once a shared haven, now felt emptier than ever. The silence in the house answered my questions. I was there ringing in my mind, but I wasn't just asking. It struck me as ironic—while he was enjoying Bora Bora, I was left to deal with everyday life, constantly aware that he was unavailable.

Sixteen days might not seem long, but without a loved one, it can feel much longer. His being so far away made the emotional distance in our relationship feel even more real. The days went by, and I kept realizing that if I had a problem or needed him, he wouldn't be there. In fact, he was never there. Ten days had passed since Max unexpectedly left for Bora Bora, suddenly changing the course of our lives. On the tenth day, my phone rang, breaking the quiet routine I had settled into.

The ringtone rang out, and when I answered, I heard something I hadn't in a long time: "I love you." The words felt familiar but also confusing. At first, I couldn't believe it. I wondered if I had misheard or if the words weren't meant for me. "Who's this?" I asked, my voice a mix of surprise and amusement. "What do you mean? It's Max," he said, the conviction in his voice betraying no hint of doubt. The shock of his declaration left me momentarily speechless, a mixture of surprise and confusion swirling within me. How could this be? He had left for Bora Bora, fully prepared to be without any means of communication. Yet here he was, his voice reaching me from across oceans and miles.

The questions came quickly, one after another, as I tried to understand what was happening. How was he calling when he had assured me that signals would be non-existent? The answer, when it came, was unexpected and laced with vulnerability. He had fallen sick. His voice, no longer distant but very much present, carried a plea that tugged at my heartstrings. He needed me, and in his time of vulnerability, the lines that had divided our roles blurred. The tone was like a child asking for comfort from a parent, reminding me of the complicated nature of our relationship.

I wanted to help him, but I also felt resentful. When he told me he was sick, I couldn't help but roll my eyes inside. Of course, I should've known that he needed something. He was unreachable on his journey until he needed me to do something for him, and then he had no trouble reaching out to me.

As was with every other thing in our marriage, I was responsible for most of the things around the house, including cleaning up after Max. One day, I was going through his jacket's pockets to remove any money or other things that might get ruined in the wash before sending off clothes to the cleaners. In one of the pockets, I found a card with an interior designer's number on it. Something came over me, and before I knew it, I was dialing the number.

The ringing stopped when someone answered; it was a woman. Since I was Max's wife, she assumed I already knew everything and told me that Max was having a place which I was not aware of in Manhattan renovated to fit his style. It made no sense to me. The words felt out of place, breaking the illusion I had been holding onto. The reality that Max had an apartment that I knew nothing about was a jarring reminder of the secrets that can exist within even the closest of relationships. As I tried to understand what this meant, I realized I had to make a choice: face the truth or keep ignoring it.

I went to Max to ask him about the apartment. He told me it was supposed to be merely a "pied-à-terre," which did not sound believable to me since Max's business was in New Jersey and we lived in the suburbs of New Jersey, so there really was no need for a recreational second place.

To confirm the suspicions that had taken root in my mind, I decided to poke around myself and find out the truth. It turned out that this wasn't the only secret place.

The confrontation was tense, full of things left unsaid and the feeling of betrayal. With a heavy heart, I brought up the topic, my voice steady but with an unexpected vulnerability. The truth came out, shocking and painful to hear. But there was more to it, something I had sensed deep down. He admitted to having cheated on me, his actions a sharp contrast to the promises that had once been made under the sun-soaked skies of Bora Bora on the phone call. What was worse was that he expected me to just live with the knowledge that my husband was having flings with multiple women and felt no remorse whatsoever.

The news affected our relationship, breaking the trust and partnership that had already been weakened by everything we had gone through. The girl he was involved with was in her twenties, a stark reminder of the passage of time and the changes that come with it. The age difference showed the growing distance between us, a gap that became clear when faced with the truth.

I couldn't believe it. We had been married for fifteen years at that point, and our sex life had been dormant for several of those. There was a period in time when I had suspected that maybe my husband was gay and was, therefore, no longer interested in me. I had never thought that while I was busy raising my daughter virtually alone, he had found other women to take care of his sexual needs. In retrospect, it was a naïve move on my part, given how his previous marriage had ended, but I had chosen to have faith in him anyway.

There were more discoveries to be made. It turns out he was there, at Bora Bora, with his latest "Mistress." She was half his age and certainly not capable of being of any help to him when he was sick. She was never paid in a monetary form but rather via trips, clothing, jewelry, fancy lunches and dinners, and a lifetime membership to an exclusive spa at the Peninsula Hotel in Manhattan.

This was Max's way of not having to think that he was paying to have his needs met. They also had a sexual relationship since she had questionable morals. She was already married to a man older than my husband. The two of them eventually were arrested for a scam they ran in the exclusive Hamptons on Long Island. I believe her husband went to jail for a while, but because she had a couple of children at the time, she had been able to avoid any jail time. She had not been the only one, either; prior to her, there were others.

I should have known something was wrong when he returned from his trip to Bora Bora with much more expensive luggage than what I had packed for him. When I asked about it, he avoided answering and told me, "Don't you start," just like he always did. He had bought his "girlfriend" expensive gifts from Bora Bora, while the only thing I got was a scarf. It hurt to realize that he had spent so much on her while it seemed like I no longer mattered to him. It was a clear sign of how our relationship had changed. The truth shattered the little trust I had left, replacing it with a deep sense of disappointment. The future we once saw together was now completely changed, and I had to deal with the consequences of his actions and my own feelings. Standing there, I faced the reality that everything I had believed in was broken, and it was hard to accept.

The news hit me hard, upsetting everything in my life and leaving me uncertain about what to do next. The marriage I had believed in, the partnership I had invested my heart and soul in, had been eclipsed by the shadows of deception. As I looked at everything I had believed in falling apart, I struggled to accept it, feeling overwhelmed by disbelief.

After finding out the truth, I was stuck, doubtful of what to do next. I felt confused, angry, and sad all at once, and I didn't know how to sort through it. Everything I thought I knew had been turned upside down, and I had to figure out how to move on with the hurt of betrayal weighing on me. In the middle of all my emotions, one thing was clear—I wasn't ready to let go. Even though the situation was painful, it didn't immediately make me think about ending the marriage. It may sound strange, but the idea of divorce felt impossible. I had been through it before, and the pain from that experience still stayed with me. The thought of going through it again, of breaking apart a life we had built together, was too much for me to handle.

Even though the truth had shaken my trust and security, I found myself stuck in a place of indecision. I didn't take immediate action or ask for a separation. Instead, I stayed in a state of emotional uncertainty, torn between wanting the truth and fearing the changes it might bring. My feelings were even more complicated because of our past, which had been full of both pain and brief moments of happiness. As I dealt with these emotions, I realized that my situation was a reflection of how complicated relationships can be. Love and disappointment, hope and fear, dreams and reality all mixed together. My choice to stay, despite the betrayal, wasn't because I was blindly loyal but because I understood how complex my life and feelings were.

I found myself at a difficult point, caught between wanting to save what was left of our relationship and the painful memories of the past. The future felt unclear, but I knew my journey wasn't over. What had once seemed like a clear path now felt confusing, mixing love, forgiveness, pain, and disappointment all together.

Chapter 8

The days passed quietly, filled with tension that felt heavy. The air, which used to be filled with shared moments and laughter, now felt uncertain and full of unspoken thoughts. Max's actions didn't seem to carry shame, but they left us feeling distant from each other. My need to please and be careful in our relationship only made the gap between us grow, a silence that needed to be addressed. I made more discoveries about the entire cheating fiasco. All of his friends had apparently known about his young girlfriend since he always took her everywhere with him and introduced her to everyone — she was half his age, as all his other young girlfriends had been, which gave him a sense of superiority over them.

I was scared of finding proof of his infidelity in the world around me, such as in places where they went out to eat or hang out or did other things, and each time that I unintentionally did, it would break my heart all over again. I would often call the hotels he was staying at whenever he went away on 'business trips,' and they would always say something along the lines of how he and his 'wife' had already checked out.

One regular morning, I woke up to find something unusual: a single envelope resting on my nightstand. Seeing Max's handwriting on the envelope made me feel both curious and nervous. I paused for a moment, then opened it, ready to face whatever it contained. The letter revealed things about Max I hadn't known before. It listed his sexual preferences and desires, many of which were completely unfamiliar to me. The shock of reading it left me confused and unsettled. I realized he must have written it because he felt too embarrassed to say it to me directly.

I had anticipated a letter, perhaps an apology or a heartfelt attempt at justification for his actions. What I encountered, however, transcended the boundaries of my imagination—a confession, a raw admission of an affinity for S&M that ran far deeper than I could have fathomed. It was the key he offered to unlock the mystery of his infidelity, accompanied by a startling proposition—to introduce me to this world, should I choose to explore it "together." Moreover, I also found out that his "girlfriend" was a dominatrix, which is why he was with her. Everything made a lot more sense to me now.

After the initial shock and anger, I felt a strange curiosity. This wasn't just a surprise; it opened a door to a side of Max I hadn't seen before. His desires showed me a new part of who he was, and I found myself wanting to understand not just this side of him but his motivation. At first, I felt confused and unsure, trying to understand the strong emotions this new information brought up in me. But over time, my curiosity grew into a strong determination. I wanted to learn more about BDSM and understand what had drawn Max to it. With each passing day, my need to comprehend deepened, driven by a desire to learn and fix the emotional distance that had come between us.

This decision was to bring about a 180-degree change in my personality, a complete, jaw-dropping shift from the person that I used to be. I started learning about BDSM, diving into a world that felt both exciting and unfamiliar. It was a personal journey driven by a strong need to understand something I had never considered before. As someone who had always been called a "prude" and only experienced physical intimacy within the boundaries of marriage, this was a big change in how I saw things. It felt important to me, especially because of the years I had spent with Max.

I turned to books to help me understand, reading everything. I also watched movies to have a better understanding I could find about BDSM. Each book gave me new information about the different behaviors and desires within this world. I also spoke to people who shared Max's interests, and their perspectives helped me see things in a new way. I even watched movies related to the topic, trying to learn as much as I could from every source available. I wanted to understand everything, so I focused on learning about the desires and preferences I didn't know about before. It wasn't just about how things worked; I also wanted to understand why people felt this way. My curiosity pushed me to keep learning, and I couldn't stop searching for answers.

I started to look for more ways to learn, and I found a group in Manhattan called the "Eulenspiegal Society." It was a place where people with similar interests came together, a safe space where they could talk about their fantasies and explore new ideas. The group met every two weeks, and I made it a habit to go, hoping to learn from others who shared the same thoughts. Each meeting was a chance to learn more about people's desires and connections that were new to me. I watched, listened, and took mental notes to better understand this world. What stood out to me was how close the society's meetings were to Max's apartment. It felt like the more I learned, the clearer the picture of Max's life became. Max had rented the top floor of a building and made it into a luxurious space. The marble floors shone under soft lighting, and the furniture and decorations were custom-made. It showed how much effort he had put into creating a place that reflected his tastes. As

I learned more, everything started to fit together, and I felt like I was uncovering important truths in this fascinating journey.

At first, I was completely new to this world and didn't know much. But my main reason for exploring was clear: I wanted to understand the man I had been married to for years, who always seemed like a mystery to me. As I learned more, my reasons for continuing to explore began to change.

Little did I foresee that I was on the brink of a transformation, one that would ironically contradict my innate penchant for people-pleasing. The stark contrast between my carefully curated persona that came to be loved by thousands around the country for its dominating behavior and the reality of my existence as a chronic people pleaser — which was also obvious by the fact that I had done this all for Max — still amazes me to this day. Human psychology is fascinating and mesmerizing in its complexity, to say the least.

My approach to this newfound journey adopted a psychological perspective, a natural inclination considering my academic background in the subject. What fascinated me was the way powerful, successful people who controlled every part of their lives could choose to give up that control in the bedroom, finding pleasure in letting go. It was a complicated mix of power and emotions. Until now, my understanding had come from what others said and from movies, which were often influenced by the views of the filmmakers and didn't show the real experiences. To truly understand, Max suggested something unusual; he would take me to meet a Mistress with whom he was going to have a session.

The idea of my husband with another woman, especially one more experienced than me, made me feel uneasy. The thought of watching them together turned my stomach. But instead of saying no right away, I let the idea sit in my mind. Eventually, I asked myself, "Why not?" With a mix of fear and curiosity, I agreed to go with him. I clearly remember my surprise as I watched the interaction between the Mistress and my husband, even while I was in the room. I had heard about things like this before, but seeing it in person gave me a completely different perspective. In that moment, I began to understand the depth of my husband's desires and the kind of woman who truly captured his interest. As someone with a background in psychology, I couldn't help but feel curious. It was then that I decided to explore this unfamiliar world further, not just for my husband but also to learn more about myself.

That was where Mistress Raven was born.

Me as Mistress Raven

The pull of this new world was too strong to resist, and I decided to fully step into it. I created a new identity for myself, far different from my usual role as someone who always tried to please others. I called myself "Mistress Raven," taking on the persona of a dominatrix who contained control—exploring desires I had never considered before. This experience wasn't just about understanding others; it was also a way to learn more about myself. Instead of starting my own group or creating a space like the ones I had seen, I decided to take a different approach. I rented a space in a high-end establishment where I could learn from people who already had experience in this world. At 44, I carried myself with confidence and grace. If I was going to be part of this lifestyle, it would be in a way that felt right for me and different from the usual way it was done.

My transformation extended to the very core of my identity. "Mistress Raven" was more than just an alias; it was an homage to the raven-hued strands of my hair. I was determined to make my place in this new world. To do this, I advertised my services in the right publications. However, I made it clear that I was different. In my ad, I stated that I was a unique dominatrix and set a firm boundary—there would be no sexual activity involved. This decision made me stand out and showed that I was following my own rules with a clear purpose.

Mistress Raven, an unexpected sensation in the world of dominance and submission, defied convention with her unique presence. In a scene filled with young dominatrices dressed in leather, with piercings, tattoos, and whips, I was very different. My approach focused on using words, which could sometimes be more powerful than physical restraints. Humiliation was a recurring theme on the menu, accompanied by an extensive list of diverse fetishes. Each session I conducted was an exquisite custom-crafted experience tailored to the specific desires of my clients. I became the "Mistress du jour," and I was someone whose name, when mentioned, was accompanied by awe and curiosity. Over time, my popularity grew far beyond what I had expected. A fetish magazine called *Dominant Mystique*, run by a woman from Queens, featured me on its cover. This brought new opportunities, including an invitation to host events at a well-known fetish club called the Vault. I agreed, but only if it could be done my way — with class and elegance. I had custom costumes made, wrote a detailed Script, and organized an event designed to stand out in the world of fetish culture.

For this event, I planned every detail carefully. I took on the role of a modern-day Cleopatra, carried into the room on a decorated wooden platform by men dressed for the part. With rented palm trees around me, I sat on a throne, looking like someone in charge. Two men, acting as "slaves," fanned me with large palm leaves. Other Mistresses and a young man dressed in a pirate-style shirt were also part of the act. His shirt had small tears, and his arms were chained above his head. As part of the scene, the woman dramatically ripped off his shirt, preparing him for a symbolic whipping. However, I chose not to actually use the whip myself. Every aspect — lighting, music, costumes — was planned down to the smallest detail. I even changed costumes several times throughout the night to keep the experience dynamic.

My reputation grew far beyond the club, gaining attention across the country. Surprisingly, my husband also became part of this world. Writing a weekly column for the same magazine that featured me, he entered the scene as a

Slave Christian, serving as my personal submissive under the persona of Mistress Raven.

I also acted in a movie that was written by someone in the scene, and I played the character Karen Thorne, a businesswoman dealing with the challenges of life. We hired professional union workers and actors for the project professional director, who had no prior experience with S/M, learned along the way, and it was filmed in my home, which had been featured in Elle Décor magazine. The filming was intense and finished in just nine days. During that time, I barely slept and even came close to getting pneumonia. Despite the challenges, I felt a deep sense of pride and happiness, knowing how unexpected and unique this experience had been in my life.

Chapter 9

In my unique line of work, I found my background in acting to be an unexpected asset. I wasn't performing on a grand stage or reading lines from a script, but my craft involved a different kind of roleplay, one that needed a sense of drama and the ability to imagine exciting stories. My talent was in a different kind of theater, one hidden in secrecy, where I created deep stories rooted in desire. I was skilled at pretending and a master of hidden craft.

To set the stage for these performances, I got a special landline, a direct link to the world of imagination. Clients followed a simple rule. They call that number to make an appointment where their unfulfilled needs would be met. In these secret meetings, their hidden fetishes were addressed. I was the choreographer, the director, and the producer. I never met clients in the evenings, only during the daytime when my assistant was present.

Living in a wealthy gated community, we needed a perfect cover story, something that wouldn't raise any questions, so we decided I would pretend to be a financial consultant—a simple and believable role. The poor guard at the gatehouse had no idea that the people coming to our place weren't looking for financial advice. He was completely clueless about the unusual kind of "consultation" they were actually seeking.

An ad for my services

Every star needs a loyal helper, and I was no different. My housekeeper, who used to stay in the background, now took on an important role as my trusted partner. She was the unsung luminary of our covert production, orchestrating behind-the-scenes intricacies with deft precision.

When our excited guests arrived at the gate, the guard had them drive to my home. My assistant would greet them at the door, escort them at the door, bring them to the living room, and have them seated on the couch. Classical music playing in the background made a comfortable environment to be in.

Once inside, our visitors would step into a world of illusion, our living room meticulously adorned to evoke a mood of enchantment and enigma. Greetings were exchanged with an understated sardonic charm as if conveying, "Welcome to the performance." A glass of wine would appear in their hand while soft, tempting music filled the room, creating the perfect atmosphere for the day's captivating event.

My house stood tall, a three-story abode of secrets and desires. In the depths of its lowest floor, what was once a movie theater was transformed into a hidden chamber of hedonism, all thanks to Max's "generous" investment of fifty to sixty thousand dollars (most of which was, of course, my money). On the outside, it seemed like a place for watching movies, but beneath the surface was an entrance to a world of many possibilities. The roof and walls, cleverly designed, could move and open, exposing hidden S&M equipment. Secret doors, hard to spot unless you knew where to look, were waiting to be found.

As I walked down the grand staircase, each step filled with excitement, I put on a sleek black trench coat, a cloak that added to the mystery of what was about to happen. At the heart of this transformative performance, I welcomed my guests into the living room, my eyes veiled in mystery.

Seated before the flickering fireplace, I adopted the role of both interrogator and confidante.

With a notebook in hand, I set out to explore their thoughts, digging into the deepest corners of their desires. Questions flowed like the fine wine I served, probing their very essence. I tried to understand the mysteries of their desires, figuring out the complex language of their preferences. It was basically "topping from the bottom," which meant that the Mistress would do what the clients wanted her to perform. In reality, every act is intended to fulfill their desires and needs. Verbal abuse, a mix of words that hurt and sparked interest, was common in my space and something I was good at, as I learned their weaknesses and used them to fulfill their needs. The attraction to physical punishment, a blend of pleasure and pain, called to them. And then there was the roleplay, where fantasies came to life.

Like a psychologist, I carefully explored the depths of their minds. Their desires, flaws, and cravings resonated in my thoughts. I confirmed their likes, sensing the subtle power dynamic between us. With a small signal to my assistant, I told her to begin. Down in our redesigned space, she took charge of the change. The lights, dim and appealing, set the mood while the music, with its seductive beat, filled the air. The hidden equipment appeared, each item reflecting our shared fantasies.

Going deeper into the space, I let go of the role of Brittany, the housewife looking for approval, and became Mistress Raven. With each step, I left behind the mundane and took on the extraordinary. In the dim space of the room, I became the symbol of power and control, a creator of pleasure and a Mistress of desire. The room was no longer just a place for secrets; it was a stage for freedom, where suppressed desires could be expressed. Compared to my real self, it was almost ironic.

In this different world of secrecy and longing, a special bond often develops between dominants and their loyal submissives. It's a connection built in the hidden parts of the mind, where secret wishes and unexpressed needs find a safe place. For the submissive, it's an act of deep trust. They share their most personal desires with their Mistress, showing weaknesses they wouldn't share with anyone else, not even a close friend or spouse. For the dominants, it's about keeping that trust and making sure the submissive's needs are met, putting their partner's desires above their own.

The attraction of giving up control is not just about surrendering power; it's about letting go of fear—fear of being judged, ashamed, or rejected. In the sacred space created between a mistress and a submissive, they both find acceptance, understanding, and freedom to be their most authentic selves. As the Mistress, I was not merely an enactor of fantasies; I was a keeper of secrets, a guardian of their hidden desires.

Over time, this profound trust often transcended the boundaries of the dungeon. It grew into something deeper, something that words like "love" tried to describe but never quite could. Some submissives found the courage to express their feelings openly, while others, overcome by shyness, kept their emotions veiled.

Among those who fell in love, a British gentleman stood out, addressing himself as "Princess" due to his fascination with femininity. In his eyes, I became everything he wanted, and he expressed his feelings through love letters and a flood of red heart emojis. In his writing, he opened up his heart. Because of the distance between us, his true desire is to serve me full-time.

A man in New York daily composes love poems in French that arrive like clockwork. We talk every day, and sometimes, he sends me video clips and sings love songs, inserting my name within the lyrics. These expressions were the manifestations of a connection that stretched beyond the physical, bridging the distance between us.

Then, there was an interesting situation with a British client, who, without knowing, was talking to someone nine years older than him when I was a private Mistress in New Jersey. Our encounters were cloaked in role-play, the scenarios shifting like sands in the wind. He traveled the world for his diamond business, and for two years, our lives intertwined within these carefully crafted narratives.

I would write a mini script with characters and a storyline different for each scenario. In the two hours that he spent with me, he only wanted roleplay, which lasted two years. I kept my true identity hidden so his fantasy could feel real, but it came with a small cost: the effort of denying his affection outside our special relationship and the understanding that, no matter how great it was, we could never be together.

Men chauffeuring me around the city.

He was charming, funny, and definitely attractive. During these secret meetings, he fell in love. Phone calls from distant planes and London homes testified to the depth of his adoration. He even dared to invite me to lunch, and as we drove to my gated community, his hand found mine. It was a brief moment of closeness that brought up feelings I had to push down because of my marriage and the fact that the guard knew me as a financial advisor, not as I truly was.

Eventually, the boundaries between fantasy and reality blurred, and the time came for truth to emerge. I unveiled my real name, my marital status, and the existence of my daughter. In return, he confided his true identity — married, with a young son. This may seem odd to most people, but in our world, it shows the trust and loyalty that developed between two individuals, connected not just by their wants but by the strong bond they created in secret.

The sudden dive into the intriguing world of S&M transformed my life from dull and empty to exciting and full of energy. It became the centrifugal force of my existence, seamlessly merging with my professional endeavors, social escapades, and intimate world. Yet, its' strong presence didn't stop my husband from having affairs, a contrast that highlighted the complexity of our relationship.

Come Sundays, a distinct transformation would unfold within the walls of our home. These were the days when my husband and I would indulge in S&M ourselves. On the surface, I was meant to take on the role of the dominatrix, the one in control and authority. This was the world where I was supposed to rule. But this was the paradox and the root cause of my newfound interest: even though I was seemingly the one in charge, it was always me submitting to my husband's desires and never the other way around, which was true of more things than just our sex life.

Two years had elapsed since I made the pivotal decision to associate myself and indulge in a dominatrix lifestyle. On one fateful day, a client awaited my attention downstairs, the anticipation of our rendezvous hanging heavy in the air. As I sat in the bathroom, perched on the dresser, contemplating the path I had forged, I couldn't help but feel like the pillar supporting the weight of our existence was a charade.

Simply expressing my wish to leave this secret world sent my husband into a fit of rage. His anger was intense, like a storm approaching, and the life we had built on these complex desires was now at risk.

After much contemplation and soul-searching, Max suggested we open a facility in Manhattan. He asked his partners to invest in his $25,000. I agreed only if it was elegant and sophisticated and met my standards. A new journey, one that would turn our secret affairs into something bigger and more refined. Since I was no longer open to the idea of being a mistress, Max proposed the idea of opening an elegant and cultured sex club right in the heart of New Jersey. With the backing of investors from our packaging company, who readily poured a quarter of a million dollars into this endeavor, our vision began to take shape.

We decided to lease a quite large top floor in a building on 18th Street and Fifth Avenue. We, along with a professional decorator, designed a fantastical haven for our clients. I had an office there as well. It was run exactly as a business.

My vision for this enterprise was clear, and my requirements for the women we intended to hire were stringent. They had to possess a college degree, and they had to be newcomers to the industry, unburdened by preconceived notions or routines. My intention was to not only provide pleasure but to educate and empower these women in the art of sensuality. I didn't want to be a mistress and see clients anymore, but that did not mean I wanted my refined knowledge of this art to go to waste.

I had advertised "a club opening," specifically not stating what kind of club—I didn't want someone who already had their own idea of how they operated in this line of work because I wanted my employees to be purely trained in my ways. With the help of a trusted friend and a woman whom I had as my assistant, we interviewed women who answered the ad that was placed in the newspaper, searching for prospective candidates by looking at people who had replied to my ad and filtering out the ones we did not find suitable.

This diligent friend would locate potential recruits, bringing them to a discreet restaurant where I would conduct thorough interviews. These conversations explored their backgrounds, dreams, and wants, helping me decide if they were right for our unique arrangement. For those who met my high standards, the process continued, ending with paperwork that officially brought them into our world.

It was through these meticulous processes and Max's firm commitment that Pandora's Box was born—a haven for the exploration of desires and the embodiment of fantasies. Referred to by some as "the Disneyland of S/M" due to its collection of themed rooms, our creation became a place of pleasure and elegance in the heart of the city that never sleeps.

Chapter 10

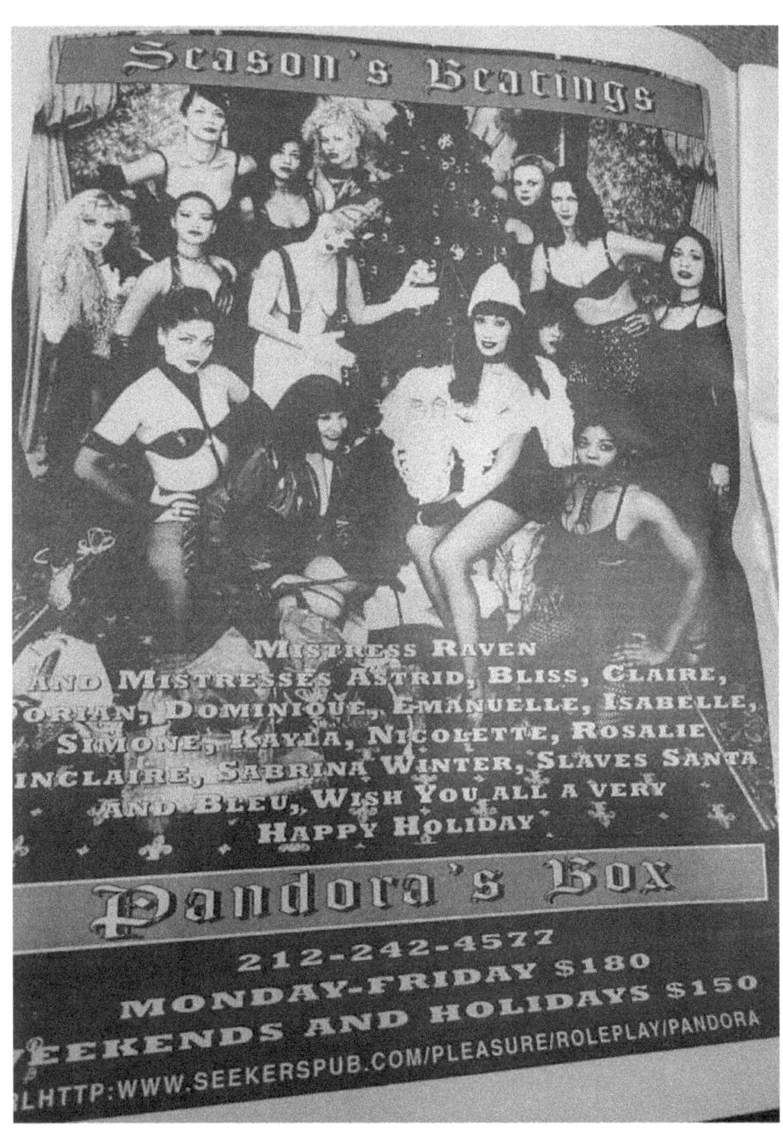

Season's Beatings
MISTRESS RAVEN
AND MISTRESSES ASTRID, BLISS, CLAIRE,
DORIAN, DOMINIQUE, EMANUELLE, ISABELLE,
SIMONE, KAYLA, NICOLETTE, ROSALIE
SINCLAIRE, SABRINA WINTER, SLAVES SANTA
AND BLEU, WISH YOU ALL A VERY
HAPPY HOLIDAY
Pandora's Box
212-242-4577
MONDAY-FRIDAY $180
WEEKENDS AND HOLIDAYS $150
HTTP:WWW.SEEKERSPUB.COM/PLEASURE/ROLEPLAY/PANDORA

About three months after we introduced the exciting world of Pandora's Box to the city that never sleeps, something surprising happened. The powerhouse of storytelling, HBO, came to us, led by the famous Nick Broomfield. HBO was planning a documentary and had chosen three interesting topics, one of which was the world of fetish.

Originally, HBO had envisioned a production that spanned the cities of Los Angeles, New York, and Tokyo, capturing the essence of these diverse landscapes. However, once Nick Broomfield, the British filmmaker extraordinaire, entered the picture, everything changed. Nick, a resident of Los Angeles, had already dipped his toes into research in the city of angels before setting his sights on the world we had crafted in New York.

When he arrived, a surprising connection was made. It felt like fate brought us together, two people united by a shared interest in the depths of desire. Nick Broomfield, with his sharp insight, decided that Pandora's Box was the perfect place to uncover the secrets of fetishism. He quickly told HBO that he wanted the documentary to focus entirely on our establishment. So, the stage was set for something special. The days that followed were incredible. For Nick, our space of sensuality became both the canvas and the subject. The work was tiring, but I was overwhelmed by a strong love for the project.

structed to visit this woman Karen Thorne and obtain from her by any means possible a signature of proxy regarding her holdings in the corporation. The son is hesitant to comply, preferring instead to berate the father with recriminations regarding the father's treatment of the deceased wife and mother. It is eventually settles that the son will undertake the assignment and he sets off to visit Ms. Thorne.

The young man realizes almost instantaneously that he is into something far beyond his ability to understand and control. He is, however, uncertain of its nature or why it holds such an attraction for him. Ms. Thorne continually interrupts her time with this neophyte to attend to the other pets strewn about in the various enclosures and alcoves of her home. We get to observe her interactions with these worthless indivi-duals who exist only for her pleasure and enjoyment. She opens a secret closet in which a slave is restrained, and as she amuses herself watching him., she summons the butler to bring her wine. When the tuxedo clad servant returns with the wine on a tray of silver, she removes that glass and delicately sips from it as the parched man tied before pleads with his eyes for some taste of moisture. She asks if he wishes to imbibe, and when he leans forward in a feeble attempt to partake, she pours the rich red liquid onto the floor in front of him. He slumps backward in total resignation to his fate and the Mistress appears at once angry by this disrespect as she turns and spits in the face of the submissive. Finished, she again encloses him in the column of faux marble completely out of sight and sound of anyone. Only she knows he exists.

After we are treated to a quick glimpse of a man suspended in a harness hanging on an attachment from the ceiling with a face straight out of Beauty and the Beast, she returns to the next level where she begins her interrogation of the young executive. It is subtle and the man is confused by the double ententes'. She indicates to him that "Most men do what I want", to which he replies, "I know", but she refuses to let this opportu-

A snippet of the article in "Village Voice."

The documentary was a huge success even before it was shown on HBO. It was played at film festivals all over the world and, afterward, was shown in an artsy film theater in Manhattan. It became one of the major forces behind my subsequent rise to fame for a few years—I received phone calls from places around the globe for interviews and also from the famous Village Voice in NY.

Back in the days that I was still seeing clients, quite a few years before the opening of Pandora's Box, I made a film named "Submission" within the confines of my own residence. The filming sessions lasted a tough twelve hours a day, leaving me with only four hours of rest each night. Still, despite the physical and mental tiredness, there was a strong drive that kept me going through every shot.

However, as fate would have it, the story took an unexpected twist. The distributor, who was in charge of the master copy of my creation, suddenly disappeared, with their last known location in the far-off Midwest. This turn of events was a cruel blow, one that might have devastated many. Even in this difficult situation, there was a small ray of hope. My husband had a copy of the film. It's still with us, but it's not very useful without the master copy.

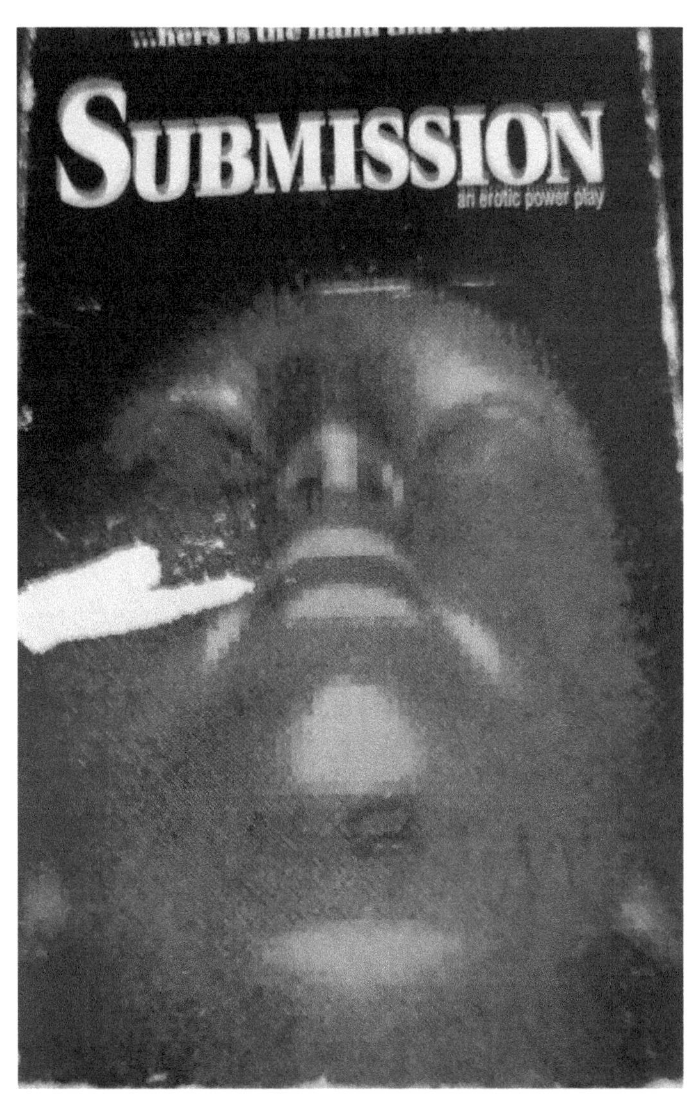

Cover of my movie, Submission

Cover of a book compilation of still photographs from my movie, Submission, taken by the famous photographer Susan Meiselas.

I also want to mention the traumatic event I experienced on 9/11. We had moved back into Manhattan five years earlier when the attack happened. We lived four blocks from ground zero and were evacuated the next day for four days. We found out what had transpired when the police banged on our door, telling us to evacuate immediately. In ten minutes, I gathered what I could, along with my dog in a crate and cat in a carrier. Frightening.

Outside, it looked like London in the blitzkrieg. We were only allowed to walk—no transportation was permitted. My daughter lived behind the World Financial Center and was evacuated when the second plane hit. She witnessed people jumping from the buildings and landing on the ground. I cried every day until one day in November when I mentioned to my husband that I hadn't cried. The next morning, my sister called to tell me that my mother had died. She had been suffering from dementia for 12 years, so this was actually like her second death.

The PTSD from those events lasted for quite a while.

As I reminisce about those intense years, it's evident that my life has undergone significant transformations since my days as Mistress Raven and the Pandora's Box venture. One of the most notable shifts was the decision to part ways with the business, selling my shares to my partner. We parted on good terms, and as per our agreement, I still receive a weekly check with a share of the profits from the business.

Mistress Raven has retired from her role as a dominatrix, but the appeal she once had still remains in the memories of those she met. The bonds formed during those intimate and intense sessions went beyond mere client and dominatrix; they were connections that transcended the bounds of the dungeon. Even today, admirers from across the globe reach out, their declarations of love echoing through the phone lines. It is the evidence of the enduring impact of those secretive encounters and the relationships they created—a reminder that the unique world I once inhabited continues to cast its spell, no matter how far removed from it I may be now.

Until I met my husband, my life was characterized by safety and kindness. However, that all changed when we crossed paths and fell in love at the age of 28. It felt like there wasn't a day unless he was away on business or, as he would claim, work-related trips (which were often just cover-ups for his weekend escapades). Oddly, these meetings often took place on holiday weekends. Even though I had my doubts and struggled with accepting them, I would go along with his explanations.

Every day when he was at home, I was subjected to hurtful name-calling, none of which was endearing. I endured various forms of abuse, encompassing verbal, physical (although never on the face where it could be seen), mental, financial, and emotional abuse. If I ever caught him cheating, I'd be thrown to the ground and subjected to repeated kicks.

I recall one incident when I mentioned the name of his latest girlfriend. In a fit of anger, he pulled the silverware drawer out and threw it across the kitchen. He then chased me through the house and up the stairs as I ran into the bathroom, locking the door behind me. I pretended to call the police while he knocked on the door nonstop. My heart raced, but I remained paralyzed by fear, though I can't quite explain why. There are countless occasions like this one—evictions, periods of homelessness, panic attacks—all while therapists and everyone I knew urged me to leave him.

The fear of what might happen, along with my past divorce and knowing how spiteful my husband could be, made me hold onto the hope that things would get better. Love still lingered within me, even though, as a psychology major, I recognized that my husband was essentially an insecure man-child. He needed me more than he loved me, a dynamic that persists to this day. Don't get me wrong—we love each other, but I was the one who bore the brunt of the actions of his troubled psyche. My time as a dominatrix was an unexpected but welcome escape from my difficult life.

Looking back on the strange path my life took, I can't help but notice the irony. For as long as I can remember, I've always tried to please others, focusing on meeting their needs and wants. I found happiness in making others happy, often neglecting my own needs. I played this role so well that I almost forgot who I really was, hidden behind the image of the perfect daughter and housewife.

And then, there was the Mistress Raven persona, a dominatrix who commanded and controlled, a stark contrast to the woman who had spent a lifetime yielding to the whims of others. It was a role I never planned to take on, but it came to me, or maybe I discovered it, and it gave me the chance to explore a part of myself that I had kept hidden for a long time.

The irony of my situation wasn't lost on me. I, who had always struggled with assertiveness in my personal life, found a newfound strength in the world of domination. In those dimly lit chambers, I was the one in control, the one giving commands and setting boundaries. It was liberating in a way that I had never imagined. I began to realize that asserting myself could be empowering and that it wasn't selfish to have desires and needs of my own.

My journey as Mistress Raven allowed me to break free from the confines of my people-pleasing tendencies and discover a form of self-expression I never knew existed. It was a path that led me through the shadows and into the light of self-discovery, where I learned that fulfilling my own desires didn't make me any less of a caring and compassionate person. In fact, it made me stronger and more authentic.

As I look back on those years, I can't help but smile at the irony of it all. The people-pleaser became the dominatrix, and in that transformation, I found a deeper understanding of myself and a newfound sense of empowerment. Life has a funny way of leading us down unexpected roads, and I'm grateful for the twists and turns that brought me to this point, where I can finally say that I've learned to balance the art of pleasing others with the importance of honoring my own desires.

Addendum

And that, dear readers, is the end of my narrative. I hope this has given you some enjoyment and maybe even helped you get to know the mistress or submissive side of yourself a bit better.

Princess first contacted me several years ago from Europe, where he was living under the delusion that he was male. What he didn't realize was that his initial attraction to me would slowly grow into an obsession that would completely take over him. It was only when he finally realized this — finally realized that he could not live another day without being close to me — that he began to start to answer his own particular vocation finally.

Normally, I would not waste my very precious time with such a slow developer. Still, the fact that Princess' emails and messages were indicative of a truly loving and totally devoted soul resonated with my totally nurturing, giving, caring, maternal character; that is, who Mistress Raven truly is deep inside.

Apart from anything, it was a lot of fun feminizing Princess. The key to unlocking his pretty little heart was getting him to appreciate just how inferior men are to women. When he finally realized that women are stronger, brighter, and better in every way than men, he started to embrace his NEED to worship and obey the superior species. Now, he yearns only to serve Mistress Raven in any way he can, making Mistress Raven's life a better place to be.

My sweet little Princess, and how lovely he looks today in his black satin dungarees with the pretty faux pearls around his neck! (I have promised him that if he pleases me before lunch, then in the afternoon, he will be allowed to wear his new catsuit, complete with the velvet ears, long tail (made from real hair from the Pacific Islands), and that tinkling little pink collar with the bell).

"Une belle pour ma belle. C'est vrai, n'est-ce pas Princesse?"

"Oui, Maîtresse."

I am finishing this book now. Perhaps my next publication could be entitled, 'The Real Princess Diaries,' which, of course, would be his biography... although, of course, all Princess ever writes about in his daily journals is Mistress Raven anyway, so his diaries would just be more books about me!

Of course, there are many, many volumes of this diary. I am la raison d'etre for Princess, his obsession! Mistress Raven is all Princess ever thinks about 24 hours a day, seven days a week, 365 days of the year. And that, of course, is how exactly it should be.

Au Revoir!